Stories From
Other Side

A Devastating Beginning
Stories From Other Side: Book 1

By Malaya Wakefield

Paperback edition ISBN: 979-8-9883482-1-4
Also available as an eBook.

Cover and interior illustrations by Malaya Wakefield.

This book is dedicated to my family. Thank you
for everything.
-M.W

Chapter One
Hidden and seeked!

Welcome to Other Side! Our travel experts have added this exclusive section to our travel book, magically designed to appear for anyone who's crossed the Great Middle into Other Side! Surprising, considering how only a small few have ever done so? Contemplate no longer, for our travel experts have spared no detail, however small, to complete our travel book and make it comprehensive and enjoyable to all spirits! What's a spirit, you may ask? Beings made of magic that inhabit our wonderful world of Other Side, each tied to one of the four elements: Air, Fire, Water, and Earth! There are limitless variations and species for all spirits, but below is a short breakdown of the kinds of spirits you may encounter on your trip!

Nia scanned the page for a moment, then brushed a lock of powder blue hair from her eyes. She'd reread her copy of *"Travel Guide to Other Side"* hundreds of times, but she'd never understood it's strange opening that was unique to her copy. She'd never crossed through the Great Middle- a dimension that separated Other Side from "Earth," a mysterious alternate dimension she'd learned about in school- and she didn't know of any living spirit who had. Nia sighed, and closed her book with a snap. As she did she saw her reflection in the monorail window, and wondered if the day would ever come when she'd solved the mysteries of her life; and more importantly, if she'd ever be free.

She looked away from the window. Sitting in front of her Enjo was seated with his red wings curled around him, chewing on a wisp of his white hair blankly. Next to him Namei was reclined across the seat like a large serpent. The grey scales covering her wingless back shined in the light of the evening sun, and the light reflecting off of them gave her seat a faint glow. Their seats were covered with a blanket of vines naturally growing all over the walls and floor of the coach, and whenever Enjo fidgeted or moved his wings a pink blossom spat pollen into the air. Enjo repeatedly sneezing into his handkerchief was becoming unbearable, and Nia was almost looking forward to arriving at their destination.

Namei looked to Nia and Enjo, and the two of them looked back expectantly.

"Uniform check."

Automatically Nia and Enjo sat up straight and pulled on the hoods of their grey cloaks. Namei looked Nia's uniform over with a careful and searching eye typical for an adult dragon, then paused. "What did you get on the Delta?" She asked. Nia glanced to the triangle- the mathematical symbol for "delta," or change, and the Paradox's official emblem- stitched into the bottom of her cloak. A milky splatter covered up most of it, and she rubbed a finger across it. The stain didn't come off.

"Blood," She said, having no idea what it really was.

Namei grunted. "Nia, you shouldn't be so careless," She started. "Take better care of your uniform and we won't be having this conversation again."

Nia folded her arms, and scowled. Namei's gaze turned to Enjo, and she gave him a sniff.

After a pause she said, "Enjo, you smell like a fifteen-year old Harpy."

Enjo looked to Namei for a "But that should be expected," but instead her eyes glittered with annoyance.

"The hideout we're going to infiltrate has been abandoned for years, but now some rogue operatives are using it as a lair," Namei went on.

Ugh, another mission brief, Nia thought.

"Rogue operatives? You mean they left the Paradox?" Enjo asked.

"That's right. We think they stole the records they were supposed to be guarding to sell them- most likely to a reporter or something. It's our job to get them back before they're read, and if they were read," She shifted her claws. "Well, you kids know what to do. Moving on, we need to talk about the papers we're going to retrieve. Each of them are highly classified and most are from the Superiors' private files, although some of them belong to the Great Deceiver himself."

At the mention of the Great Deceiver memories flashed before Nia's eyes: nightmarish beasts chasing her and Enjo through the woods, the unfeeling voice that'd given the impossible price of her and Enjo's freedom. Rage flickered inside her, and she absently touched one of the sheathed daggers on her belt. Namei continued, "The Superior that assigned us this mission said that no one was to read them except me, since I'm the only one who can organize and ship the records to them. So once we have them, no peeking." At this she hesitated, and looked to a spot on the seat beside her. There was the scent of peach and a clipboard appeared, and Namei waved away a few sparks of her magic before reading off of it. "'The building is an underground Paradox hideout, but it was abandoned years ago due to hazardous conditions. We believe that the rogue operatives have chosen this location because of it's capabilities for lockdown, which would delay any assigned operatives entry. The hideout itself is located under a manhole cover in the industrial district with the Paradox's emblem.' Another thing. All of the spirits are armed, so hold back and you *will* die," She said, giving Enjo a purposeful glance. "That goes for you as well, Nia. Show no mercy. And if the need arises-" Namei clenched one of her forefeet over her heart, and pretended to gag.

Nia's eyes flashed with displeasure, but she didn't protest. She knew exactly what that gesture meant, and it brought back graphic memories.

"Moving on, we won't have much time. As soon as we arrive in the station near the industrial district we'll only have a twenty minute window to find the hideout, infiltrate it, and get the records." Namei tore off two other pages of her notepad, and handed them to Nia and Enjo. "I wrote further details about your roles in this mission. Any questions?"

Enjo was quiet, but his wings noticeably drooped.

"Enjo?"

He blinked in surprise and hurriedly asked, "Why can't I go with Nia?"

"Because you're not quiet enough. You'll be in charge of rigging the hideout to blow. Any more questions?"

Enjo slumped in his seat, clearly disappointed. "You're just letting Nia go because she doesn't have bird feet," He muttered. He tapped his foot on the floor, and there was a *clack clack clack* as the talons on his feet hit the floor of the monorail. "Sometimes having talons is so inconvenient," He said. "Still," He said, thoughtfully, "It *is* nice to have feet that look like a bird's, and to have feet at all, so I'm happy for them. And, plus, not *everyone* can say they have claws on their feet."

5

Nia's face lit up, and she wiggled her webbed toes. "So is having flipper feet! I mean, they look great, they help me swim faster, *and* it means I don't have to wear shoes!"

Having feet that were tough enough to never need shoes- and the fact they could always walk around barefoot unless it was cold- had been, for years, one of Nia and Enjo's favorite things to discuss. It was also one of the few things that was guaranteed to put Nia in a good mood.

Namei looked at the both of them stiffly, then asked again, "Any more questions?"

There were none.

"Well, you know what that means. Hail Eris."

"Hail Eris, and may change guide us through the dark," Nia and Enjo responded, automatically.

A squealing noise filled the following silence, announcing their arrival in the industrial district.

Ten minutes later, Nia was playing a dangerous game. Namei had pried open a manhole cover with a triangle stamped onto it, and afterwards Nia had dropped through. She landed in a dark, damp hallway, and quickly kept her footing to avoid falling on the slick floor. Her bare feet felt warm and wet, and the webbing between her toes that helped her when she swam stuck to a sticky brown liquid coating the floors. Nia quickly walked away from the foul liquid, making a mental note to wash her feet as soon as they got home. She snuck quickly through the hall, mentally keeping track of time and following the route through the hideout that Namei had instructed her before she'd gone inside. The hideout was already beginning to fill with the thick, nauseous purple gas Namei was diffusing throughout the underground lair, and she made sure her mask- which had both a headset for communication with Namei and Enjo and a layer that protected her from poisonous gas- was pulled over her mouth and nose snugly. She crawled into a vent that was rapidly filling with gas from the street level. Her eyes stung, and her vision blurred. *I haven't breathed it in so it can't hurt me. I haven't breathed it in so it can't hurt me,* she repeated to herself. After a few minutes of crawling through the vent space, and finally found a vent cover that was brightly lit from behind from a room deep in the hideout. After rattling it the thing broke in her hands, and she squeezed through the gap. She dropped through feet first, and landed onto a rafter. She dropped from the rafters onto the floor into a crouch, and held her mask close to her face. Speaking into the small microphone imbedded in it she asked, "Enjo, are you ready?"

The radio crackled. *"Yes, I'm ready. Tell me when it's time."*

"Okay. I'm getting close to the box now."

The poisonous smoke Namei had fed into the room was thick enough to obscure her vision, so she nearly tripped over a spirit lying unconscious on the floor. Nia stepped over them and approached a large safe bound with cords in one corner of the room. She pulled out one of her daggers from it's sheath on her belt. After cutting through the thick cords that was wrapped around it she looked over the safe's door with a trained eye. Enjo's voice crackled to life in her headset. *"Nia, what's taking so long? Namei can't keep this up!"*

"It's the safe. The gap between the safe and it's door is too small for me to wedge my knife between it. Just let me use my magic."

Nia uncorked the bottle she kept strapped to her belt, and directed her magic to her fingertips. She felt her own magic latch onto the presence of the water inside the bottle. Bubbles of water floated upwards, and she directed them to the outline of the safe door. They penetrated the minuscule gap between the door and the safe and expanded. A moment later the door blew off it's hinges with a satisfying crack, and Nia knelt down to look inside. In it was a clear bag filled with paper. She thrust her hand inside and grabbed it, then tucked it into her satchel. Then she turned and jumped, pulling herself onto one of the rafters. She threw her leg over it and stood. After balancing for a moment, she jumped across the beams to the vent she'd entered. Behind her she could hear the spirits beginning to stir.

"Enjo! Start the fire, *now!*"

"Now? You didn't even come out yet!"

"Just start it!"

Nia scrambled through the vents as fast as she could and down the hallway, and after half-climbing, half-jumping up the ladder through the manhole cover she threw herself out of the hideout. Beside her and a few feet away Enjo took a deep breath, then exhaled- and the breath he exhaled erupted into flame. It flew through another manhole that fed into the hideout, and orange light flashed in the darkness.

Nia stood up and grabbed Enjo's arm. "Enjo, let's go!" The two of them raced out of the alleyway onto a back street. In front of them two spirits rushed into the street and turned to face them, and instinctively Nia and Enjo stopped. The spirits raised their weapons and lunged at them, but before they could react Namei stepped from the shadows and pinned one of the spirits under her claws. She let out an ear-splitting roar. Enjo quickly looked away, but Nia couldn't. Namei's claws stabbed deep into the spirit's torso, a scream of pain pierced Nia's ears, and pearlescent blood gushed onto the ground. The other spirit gasped. *"Jeremy! No!"*

They lunged at Namei, but before their sword could reach her she spat a short, fiery breath in their eyes. A puff of nauseous gas billowed into their face and they collapsed. A moment later, both spirits were lying at Namei's feet, dead. Two glowing deathlights rose from their bodies and into the sky, and disappeared from sight. Nia watched them go with a flicker of sadness, until she remembered that if Namei hadn't stepped in, the deathlights would've belonged to her and Enjo.

Namei turned to them. "Nia, did you get the records?"

"Yep, I got them."

"Give them to me!" She snapped. Nia hastily offered the wad of papers to Namei, and they vanished in a puff of her magic.

"Enjo, is the hideout ready to blow?"

"Yes, we need to go! Now!"

"Good, then what're you kids waiting for?! Head out!" Namei barked.

Nia's eyes lingered on the two dead spirits, then she turned and ran. They raced through the streets of the crowded stretch of the industrial district, pushing past dragons carrying slabs of metal on their backs and leaping over carts filled with huge snails. The three of them didn't slow when they reached the monorail station, and as they hurried up it's polished steps, there was an explosion that rocked the industrial district.

The ride back to their apartment was silent. Their assignment was quickly fading from Nia's mind, and as she stared down at the grey outline of a triangle on her right palm, the only thing that reminded her of the deaths of the former Paradox operatives was the faint clamor of emergency bells in the distance. The triangle on her palm was red and raw from all of Nia's attempts to scrub or even burn it off, but even after two years of trying, the Delta that bound her to the Paradox was still there.

Nia scowled at it, then pulled on her gloves. She looked up just as Namei cleared her throat and said, "Kids, the assignment was a success. But, if I hadn't been there to save your necks you two would be dead. Dead! I told you to use your spirit-magic in an emergency before the assignment, didn't I?" She snarled, addressing Nia. Nia shot her a glare. "You stepped in before me or Enjo could react. And anyway, I don't care how many times you tell me to do it. I won't."

"And why's that?"

"It feels wrong. I hate it."

"If you can't handle having the power to control spirits at will you shouldn't even have it!" Her dangerous gaze turned to Enjo, and he shrunk in his seat.

"Enjo, if you can't learn to defend yourself either, you won't live to see next week! I won't always be there to save your hides, got it?!"

When Namei was finished the silence returned, and wasn't broken until a familiar announcement over the intercom signaled their return to Central Station.

Later that night, Enjo and Namei were already eating their soup at the dining table when Nia sat down to join them. She ate her first bowl without a word, and when she sat down to her second Namei asked, "So, how are you two doing?"

Her bad mood from earlier had disappeared, like it always did, and she had returned to her usual post-mission cheerfulness.

At the question Enjo kept his head low over his bowl. Nia traced the faded patchwork on the tablecloth with her spoon, glanced over at Namei, and shrugged. Her food felt heavier in her throat all of a sudden.

Namei was quiet. Then she asked, "What was the price of you two getting out of the Paradox again?"

Nia exchanged glances with Enjo, and neither of them answered.

"Hm. Not very chatty tonight," Namei mused, addressing Nia. "Out of character for you to not go on one of your angry rants about how you'll escape the Paradox."

Nia gave her a freezing glare, and put down her spoon. Enjo looked from her to Namei, and started quickly gulping down his soup in case Nia decided to flip the table over.

"Namei? Where are the papers now?" He asked after his bowl was drained, seeming eager to change the subject.

"In my room. I need to sort through them and get them labeled before they're delivered to headquarters." Namei answered.

"What if someone tries to steal them when we're asleep?"

"That's not likely."

"But what about those spirits that broke in last week?"

Nia glanced to Namei. Her expression hardened at the mention of last week's break-in, and she ate her soup delicately before replying.

"Enjo, Nia, please forget that. They were burglars."

"But... we don't have anything worth *stealing*," Enjo said.

Namei shot him a glare, and he went quiet. Nia glanced around their apartment. From the tattered curtains to the cracked, mismatched bowls they were eating from, everything screamed of poverty. For the fifth time that day she thought of where she'd be living if the Paradox had never existed: A palace under the sea with sparkling columns of white coral, gleaming dolphin fountains, and a private seaweed forest. Her ancestral home; a place she'd never been, but knew of from her parents' stories. She gave a silent, happy sigh, and slowly reality returned to her. The bare lightbulb above them flickered, and she ate another spoonful of soup to prevent herself from screaming.

"Enjo, how many hours have you spent studying magic this week?" Namei asked.

He hesitated before replying, "Four." *"Four?"*

"Magic isn't my favorite subject! It's hard for me to concentrate and learn all the formulas and reactions and laws when I don't care about any of them!" Enjo answered, defensively. Namei sighed before asking, "Nia? And you?"

"Six minutes. Out of my own free will. Because I hate the Paradox and everyone in it and no, I'm not going to just blindly take orders from *you.*" Nia snarled. Namei blew two, angry puffs of purple smoke from her nose, and closed her eyes. After ten seconds she opened them again and asked, "Enjo, did you at least clean your room when we got back?"

Enjo shrugged, and when he did, one of his wingtips bumped into Nia's bowl. It toppled, and with a splash and a crash the red soup spilled over Nia's lap and onto the floor.

Nia shrieked from the scalding heat and jumped up, and both Namei and Enjo were on their feet.

"Sorry!" Enjo cried out, rushing to grab something to clean up the soup. Namei grabbed a towel from the bathroom for Nia to dry herself, and after she did, there was a bright red stain all over her clothes.

"You're not hurt, are you?" Namei asked.

"I'm fine. I'll just go change." Nia said.

As Nia was walking to her room, she noticed the door to Namei's room was standing open, and a beam of moonlight was shining from the open window onto papers scattered across her desk. Nia walked past the room, then paused. She took a few steps back, then cautiously pushed open Namei's door. She'd always wondered what the Superiors were planning, and how they maneuvered their huge influence like spiders on webs, touching threads and spinning new ones to make their plans reality, ensnaring anything unlucky enough to get in their nets.

Curiosity got the better of her, and she took a step inside and pushed the door lightly closed behind her. Nia crossed over to the desk and stepped over Namei's uniform, which she'd tossed on the floor. Stepping lightly she came right up to the desk, and looked at the paper on top. This one had a yellow sticker, which Nia knew meant "low priority." It was handwritten, and Nia couldn't understand what it meant: *Poor duckling.* After a moment of looking at it she pulled on her gloves and pushed it aside, dismissively. Then she looked at the next paper. This one had a green sticker, which Nia knew meant it had a higher priority. This one

14

was a bit more interesting. It was typed and read like a shopping list:

A token from Earth
Nightclover
The ashes of a Phoenix
The fabric of time
Red moon dust
The heart of the mountain
A Phoenix's feather
The past, present, and future of Other Side

Nia picked up the list and flipped it over. It didn't say anything else, but it felt vaguely familiar; like she'd read a list like it many times before, somewhere else.

She set down the paper, and listened. Namei's heavy footsteps and Enjo's soft ones could still be heard clearly in the main room, so Nia suspected the soup had left a stain on the carpet, which was a bad idea when it came to Paradox housing. She guessed she'd have at least five more minutes, so she sat down instinctively in the chair at the desk, pulled on her gloves, and started to sift through more of the papers.

Most of them were records of rogue operatives the Paradox had killed, others were records from the Paradox's treasury, and some were more handwritten notes like the first one she found. She suspected they'd been written by the Great Deceiver, and holding them in her hands filled her with a sense of dread. She pushed aside a record of Paradox movements in the Province of the Fire Spirits, and thought about how great it would be if these papers fell into the right hands. If these records were revealed to the world, the Paradox and all of their terrible deeds would be exposed. Then maybe the spirits of Other Side would understand how dangerous the Paradox really was, and put a stop to them.

She moved aside another paper, and looked at the one underneath it. It was laying on the direct middle of the table, the last record in the pile. It was the only paper that was marked with a bright purple sticker, which Nia had never seen before. She picked it up to see it better in the fading moonlight.

What she saw made her gasp.

Written across the top of the paper were the words: *Recreating the Devastation.*

Nia stared at the paper in shock. The chapter of her magic history textbook on the Devastation- a potion so potent three drops nearly destroyed Other Side- came back to her. She snatched the paper and, heart pounding faster with every word, quickly read the rest of it: *On Eris' Day we brew the Devastation, and wipe Other Side clean. The death of all will be the price for the New Era- the survivors: the Moon Spirits, the Cosmo Spirits, and the most loyal of the Paradox, will reclaim the world of Other Side, now a pure home to call their own. Hail Eris and bound this secret in your blood, for this is the great dream of the Paradox. May change guide you through the dark, to the light of the New Era. -Your torchbearer, Sascha Ellis: "The Great Deceiver"*

Underneath was the list Nia had read before, which she assumed was the ingredients needed for the Devastation.

Nia's mind reeled. The Paradox was planning to recreate the Devastation? On Eris' Day? Memories flashed through her minds' eye: posters promoting upcoming firework displays, discounts on all kinds of gifts, and the countless party invitations Namei had gotten in the mail and quickly hid from Nia and Enjo. Eris' Day was happening in eight days. And that meant unless something changed, in eight days, everyspirit in Other Side would die.

There was the sound of the doorknob turning, and Nia quickly snatched the paper. The door opened, and Enjo stepped into the room. He paused. "Nia? What are you doing?" He asked.

"What are *you* doing?" Nia asked.

"Namei asked me to grab her uniform from her room and put it away before our mission tomorrow morning," He said. Enjo looked past Nia. "Were you... looking at the records?" He asked, astonished. Nia scrambled for an answer. She didn't want to lie, but she didn't want to tell the truth either. So she walked over to Namei's uniform, picked it up off the floor, and thrust it into Enjo's arms.

"Please don't tell Namei," she said.

"What? *Wait- you were looking at the papers!*"

"No, I- okay, fine, I was!"

"But why? Namei said that we couldn't!"

"Who cares about what Namei says?" She snapped, bitterly.

"You're going to be in *huge* trouble if Namei finds out!"

"I know! Let's talk about this later."

"Did you touch any of them?"

"We'll talk later!" She hissed.

"Did you *take* any of them?!"

Namei's voice called out from the main room, and Nia and Enjo froze. "Nia? Enjo? What's going on?"

"Sorry!" Enjo squeaked. "It took me a long time to find your uniform!"

Nia winced. There was a short pause, and she could imagine Namei thinking how she'd left her uniform in the middle of the floor. "Well, just get it and bring it here," Namei called back. "You two can't stay up all night, we have an assignment in the morning."

"Okay!" Enjo called back, shrilly.

Nia turned, and went back to the desk. Still wearing her gloves she tidied up the papers into their original positions and walked past Enjo out of the room, and he closed the doors behind her. Nia caught the distressed look in his eye and hurried into her own room, changed out of her uniform into a new outfit, dumped her uniform in their tiny laundry room, and returned to the main room. Namei was curled on the sofa listening to music on the radio with her eyes closed. Enjo was sitting next to her, mostly hidden in his wings and reading a book. He looked tense and anxious, and she realized that was how he normally looked now.

She grabbed a book off of the shelf (titled "How to Pretend You're Reading." On it's cover was a bright yellow sticker that read "250 million copies sold!") and sat down with it. Namei half-opened her eyes, and asked. "What took you so long, Nia?"

"I- couldn't decide what I wanted to wear."

Namei nodded, and closed her eyes.

Nia glanced at the window. The skyline of Kazaki was still bright even though darkness was falling. But even though the skyline of Kazaki usually never failed to dazzle Nia, all she could think about was how it would look reduced to nothing but rubble and ashes.

Seven days, Nia thought. *Seven days until the end of the world.*

Chapter Two
Promises!

Nia could see the spirit's eyes in the darkness. Rain poured down, electrifying her skin. *"I WILL find another way to escape the Paradox! I'll never pay the price you asked!"* She yelled. Enraged, Nia grabbed onto the force of the rainwater and redirected it, hurling it in the hooded spirit's direction. The eyes vanished.

She stood there, panting, before slowly looking over her shoulder. Instead of eyes a hand emerged from the darkness. It pointed at Nia, and fear crashed over her body as she remembered.

Nia's heart began to race so fast it was hard to hear anything else.

She took a step backwards, trembling.

A feather- silky and a shade of red so vibrant it was almost glowing- landed on her nose from somewhere above her.

"Nia, we need to go!" Enjo's voice. Then the sound of a strong wing beat, and a gust of wind blew against her face, throwing back her hair and scattering it across her face. She brushed it away and held up her arm to block out the rush of air, and gasped.

The dark forest surrounding her had disappeared and been replaced with the sky. She seemed to hang there, suspended by some invisible thread as she watched her hair rise above her head and her feet and legs curl in towards her. Then her stomach seemed to be lifted out of her, and with a realization of terror she knew she was falling. Nia fell like a stone into the water and foam swallowed her. Cold enveloped her. And under her skin she felt a shudder, then her entire body seemed to become electrified with energy. She flung out her arms and legs to swim, and sunk further into the water before coming up. Gasping- not for lack of air, the nearly invisible gills on her neck took care of that- she broke the surface, and stared at the endless expanse of water around her. From somewhere far away, a thought registered. *Kasaan. The ocean.* Then the thought vanished, replaced with panic. *Enjo. Where's Enjo? Did he land in the water?*

She scanned the surface. There was nothing but the unbreakable line where the sky met the sea, and the waves that carried her up and down, washing seawater into her mouth. She licked her lips, then her eyes fluttered. Drowsily she closed her eyes, her head dipped below the surface, and she fought the urge to go to sleep. She couldn't sleep now.

There was something she had to do- something she needed to tell herself.

Wake up. Yes, wake up! She had to tell herself to wake up- why, though? Nia wasn't asleep yet. Tired, but not asleep. Her eyes fluttered again.

Wake up! It's just a dream!

With a start, Nia opened her eyes.

She woke to sunlight shining through her bedroom window, and groaned.

Ten minutes later, Namei was cooking breakfast. She'd tasked Nia and Enjo with doing the laundry and left, so the two of them were left alone in the laundry room. Since they had a mission that day they were already wearing their uniforms, and Nia had already packed her satchel and strapped on her daggers and water bottle. She had a weird feeling that she would need them soon, and she didn't like it.

Nia was taking the dirty clothes and putting them into the washing machine, and Enjo was taking dry clothes from the dryer and putting them into the clean laundry basket. He'd been anxious all morning, and Nia had been worried that Namei would get suspicious. Fortunately, however, she could hear Namei in the kitchen, singing along off-key with a song on the radio, so that seemed unlikely.

Five minutes after the door to the laundry room closed, Enjo asked anxiously,

"So? Tell me about the papers! What happened? Did you touch any? Did you take any? Did you wrinkle any?"

Nia shook her head gravely. "No, I think I got all of the papers exactly how they were on the desk before. Except... there was a paper about making the Devastation."

Enjo paused. "The Devastation?" He repeated. "Isn't that a potion?"

"Enjo, it's not *just* a potion. It's a potion that wiped out an entire province with one drop and nearly destroyed the world with three!"

"Really? When?"

"Before we were born. The Assembly reversed it, remember? Don't you remember *anything* from all those hours Namei forced us to study history?"

Enjo gave her a blank look. Nia went on, "Enjo, what do you think would happen if the *Paradox* got their hands on something like that? It would be a disaster!"

"Do you really think they'd use it to wipe out another province?"

"Of course they would, they're the *Paradox!*"

Enjo's eyes went wide, and the feathers on his wings bristled with anxiety.

"This is terrible! If three drops nearly destroyed the world, what could four drops do? Or five? Or *six?*"

He started to pace back and forth across the laundry room. "The Paradox is trying to destroy the world, we're still stuck working for them against our will, and we're the only ones who know besides the Superiors and the Great Deceiver and Namei! And Namei is still working for the Paradox even though she *knows* so we can't expect her to not want to work for the Paradox if we told her! And then she'd probably sell us out to the Superiors, and they'd tell the Great Deceiver, and then we'd be Listed, and then we'd be *dead* because all of a sudden every spirit in Other Side would be hunting us down! *Again!* And we wouldn't even be with our parents!"

"Enjo, calm down, Namei will hear us!" Nia hissed. She went on, "Look, I don't think she noticed anything, because she already sent the papers out to the Superiors. She wouldn't send it if something was wrong, because then she'd be in huge trouble, right?"

Enjo's wings, which had been tight and tensed, relaxed. "Right," he said.

"So, that means Namei didn't notice anything."

"What about the plan to make the Devastation? What if the Paradox really does use it to destroy the world? Did the paper say that was what they were trying to do?" Enjo asked.

"It said that the Paradox was going to use the Devastation to kill every spirit in Other Side in eight- well, seven now-days, on Eris' Day."

Enjo's eyes grew wider. "But why would they do that? That's horrible!"

"Maybe because they're dangerous psychopaths with no sense of spirit decency?"

"Do you think they could actually get the ingredients for the Devastation?"

"I don't know about that. The Paradox can pretty much do anything, as bad as that sounds. But some of the ingredients for the Devastation seem pretty obscure."

She repeated the list of ingredients for Enjo, and he frowned. "'The past, present, and future of Other Side?' How would they get that?" Enjo asked.

"I don't know. But I'm sure they could find a way, and that's what worries me."

"And what if they *do?* Then everyspirit in Other Side dies!"

An overwhelming feeling of hopelessness washed over Nia, and she battled with herself before answering him again.

"We need to stop them. We can't just let Other Side get destroyed."

"But where would we even start?" Enjo asked.

"I don't know. Maybe we can talk about it later," Nia answered, glancing at the clock. "Namei's probably starting to wonder what's taking us so long," She said.

She grabbed the last thing in the basket, the clothes she'd stained last night. *Namei must have separated it for some reason,* Nia thought. She picked it up, and absently flipped out the pocket for it. A crumpled piece of paper fell out onto the floor, and she and Enjo looked to it in surprise. Nia picked it up and opened it.

A chill ran over her, and she nearly dropped it. "Nia? What is it?" Enjo asked.

"It's-" Her throat went dry. "It's the paper for the Devastation," she said, quietly. Enjo looked at her in terror. "But then the Superiors are going to notice for *sure* that one of the papers is gone! And didn't you say that was the most important paper? We're going to be in so much trouble! What do you think they'll do to us?" Enjo asked.

"I- I don't know." Her stomach lurched uneasily as the door to the laundry room opened. Namei poked her head inside, and looked at them. Nia and Enjo looked back. "Hi, Nia. Hi Enjo." Namei said. The usual cheerful tone in her voice was gone, and Nia and Enjo exchanged nervous glances.

"What is it, Namei?" Nia asked.

Namei took another step into the room. There was barely enough room for the three of them in the tiny laundry room, and Nia was instantly put on edge. "Is- everything okay?" She asked.

Namei didn't answer. She stared at them with a sorrowful look, and she had her claws outstretched and shaking.

Enjo took a step back, and Nia's hand instinctively went to the water bottle she'd strapped onto her belt earlier that morning.

"Namei? Are you alright?" She asked.

A distressed look came onto Namei's face, and she put all four of her feet onto the floor. It was clear her entire body was straining from some unseen pressure building inside her.

"Nia, Enjo, I know I was assigned to look after you two because I'm good at training recruits, but I'm really happy I met you kids. Enjo, you're the sweetest and kindest kid I've ever met, and Nia- you're a brave and gifted Water Spirit. I wish there were more girls like you." As she spoke her words became more hurried. Her face contorted, and she gave a grunt of pain. "You know what's happening by now, right?"

Neither of them could speak. Then, the realization hit Nia. Everyone who volunteered (or, in Nia and Enjo's case, were forced) to join the Paradox had to sign a magical contract with their own blood- and as soon as their name was signed, the Delta would appear on their palm. It forced them to obey whatever anyone of higher rank ordered them, no matter what the request. And if the subordinate resisted, the Delta would inflict pain onto it's owner that would become so unbearable they were forced to do as the Superior asked, or die a torturous   death. "Is there a Superior here?" Nia asked. "No. They gave me this request when I volunteered to look after you two. They told me that- if you two ever learned the truth," she paused to gasp, and one of her front feet scooted towards them. Her claws raked against the tile floor. *They told me to kill you.*

Enjo's eyes went wide, and he gasped.

Nia touched the stopper for her water bottle, but didn't open it.

"Why would they want us dead if we found out the truth?" She demanded.

"I asked, but they wouldn't tell me!" Namei choked out. Her other foot went forward.

"Why did they want us to work for the Paradox in the first place?" Enjo asked, terrified.

"I don't know. I'm just an operative who signed the contract, they didn't tell me anything!" She gasped. "I really wish I knew, but I don't! Now go, get away from me! I can't resist the affects of the contract much longer!" Namei's whole body was shaking. It was clear that the strain of resisting was taking all her energy, and if she lost her focus or gave in, she'd be like a rubber band that's pulled to its limit-ready to snap with pent-up energy.

Tears were gathering in the corners of Enjo's eyes, and he stepped forward. Nia immediately grabbed him back. *"Enjo, what are you doing? Didn't you hear her?"*

Enjo's wings drooped. "I know, I just- wanted to say thank you," He said, addressing Namei. Tears streamed down his face, and he choked out, *"Thank you for looking after us. I'll remember you."*

Namei gave a pained smile, and gagged. She looked ready to spring on them any moment. "Your parents should be proud of you kids," she said, still smiling. "Now, get as far away from here as you can. Go save the world, go find your parents! *Run! And when I attack you, don't hold back!"*

She couldn't control the affects of the contract any longer. She lunged, smashing the washing machine next to Nia in one blow. Nia leaped to the other side and grabbed Enjo's arm, then dashed past Namei through the open door and into the living room. They burst into the living room and Nia threw open the sliding doors, and they ran out onto the fire escape. "Enjo, fly!" She demanded. Enjo flapped his wings twice, then gripped her shoulders with his feet. A moment later Nia kicked off the floor and felt herself lift into the air. Enjo dived off the fire escape with her in his grip, and the two of them fell ten feet before Enjo's wings spread open, and they glided low above the streets of Kazaki. Nia looked down in wonder at the crowds of spirits strolling below them and at her feet dangling in the air. Her powder blue hair blew across her face and she pushed it aside, and as she did she felt Enjo slowly begin to rise with every wingbeat. Enjo had often picked her up and flown with her like this when they were little, but that had been years ago. The same sense of wonder and excitement filled her as she looked at Kazaki from a new perspective, and she waved at the few surprised spirits who happened to look up at them. Nia was snapped out of her wonder by a sudden gust of wind from behind them, and Enjo gave a large wing beat. "She's chasing us!" He said. Nia looked back. Namei had smashed through the wall of their apartment and was now riding the wind toward them. She was flying much faster then Enjo, twisting and turning her coiled body in the air as she propelled herself forward with her Air Magic. "Enjo, you need to go faster!" Nia yelled out. They had a head start, but Namei was gaining on them at an alarming rate. It was like watching a diving falcon close in on a baby bird. "You don't think I know that?!" Enjo yelled back, pushing himself forward with every wing beat. They were rapidly climbing into the air, but they'd never be fast enough to escape Namei if Nia didn't do something. She ripped out the stopper of the water bottle strapped to her belt and quickly grabbed onto the magic of the water inside it. The water rose and moved at her will, and as Namei's claws lashed behind them so suddenly and so close they nearly took Enjo's wings off, Nia directed it. The water hit Namei in the snout, and she flinched and gagged before continuing to fly after them in pursuit. She roared, and her fangs glinted in the late morning sunlight. Nia watched as she advanced again, and this time she pulled her daggers from their sheaths on her belt. Namei drew closer for another attack, but neither she or Nia could react before Enjo's wings folded in with a snap and the two of them fell like stones. Nia shrieked as her stomach jumped into her throat, but a second later she was jerked back upwards. She looked up quickly, and past Enjo's wings she could see Namei already turning in the air to chase after them. Enjo had dropped a hundred feet before'd he opened his wings again, and now he and Nia were gliding towards a large rail. Nia quickly turned towards the sound of a loud hum, and saw a monorail blazing towards them in the distance. An idea struck her. "Enjo, fly towards the monorail!" She said. He obeyed, and they turned and coasted toward it. Nia fumbled with her satchel and grabbed a long cord with a small bag tied to it. She slipped the bag off of it's rope, and sticky black goop dripped off the end of the rope and trickled into the bag. She and Enjo had used it many times before on missions, but she'd never imagined she'd use it to escape Namei. As the monorail came closer she flung the long cord, and the sticky part stuck to the side of the monorail. At once Enjo was jerked out of the sky, and again Namei lunged at the spot they'd been before. Nia clung to the cord like it was as huge vine, paying it out but never letting go. Above her Enjo clung to her with his feet with his wings outstretched to slow their fall, and grabbed onto the cord when it came close to him. The two of them clutched the rope in a terrifying free fall, and they swung in a huge half arc.

Then the rope went taut, and Nia and Enjo were carried on by the speeding monorail. They dangled above the crowded streets of Kazaki, and a few spirits looked up at them in surprise as they passed. Namei chased after them, but not even she could catch up with the monorail's speed. Nia and Enjo were jerked around a corner as the monorail turned, and Namei disappeared behind a building. A few minutes later it pulled into a station, and the two of them let go of the rope and upwards. They flew over the monorail's roof, removed the sticky rope and covered it in its protective bag, and dropped onto the floor of the station before the doors opened for passengers.

Chapter Three
Escape!

Nia and Enjo hurried away in the crowd, and after some walking, ducked into the Jolly Bug they'd often eaten with Namei at. As Nia walked in the meaty smell of cooking lumpia welcomed her, and she took in a deep sniff. The sunny shop was empty except for Nia, Enjo, and a handful of spirits ordering takeout. They ordered two bowls of white rice with orange burk-burk meat and sat down at a table, and after a waiter gave them their food, they ate in silence. Enjo had a blank look of shock on his face, and Nia could only eat her food and wonder. Why had the Superiors ordered Namei to kill them if they'd learned the truth about the Paradox? They already knew the Paradox was horrible; but until Nia had discovered their plan to recreate the Devastation, they hadn't known *why*. A sick feeling grew in her gut, and she shoveled another forkful of rice into her mouth to distract her. She looked up at Enjo. He was poking the image of a smiling red bug- Jolly Bug, the chain's mascot- printed all over the tablecloth with his fork. *"Orenda."* He murmured. "What?" Nia asked.

He glanced up and met her eye. "It's- a word that means the power every spirit has to choose, and change themselves and the world. I've been... thinking about it a lot lately," He muttered.

He shook his head. "Never mind. What should we do now?" He asked.

"Get out of Kazaki as soon as we can. What else?"

"But how? The Paradox has spirits going on rounds around the city all the time, and they must know that we escaped."

Nia thought for a minute before answering.

"Then we escape Kazaki. Tonight. The longer we stay here, the more likely they are to find us."

"Tonight? But how are we going to get past the operatives on patrol?" Enjo asked. He didn't say it out loud, but the look in his eyes said, *And how is this escape supposed to be any different than the others?*

"I think I know how. Do you remember that assignment we went on with Namei to shut down a water taxi because the owner wasn't paying their taxes?" Nia asked.

"You mean... we *didn't* shut it down?"

"We did, but I heard some spirits talking about how it got started up again. The boat goes across the moat surrounding Kazaki, so if we can afford it, that seems like our best option, and-"

Enjo looked at Nia inquisitively, and blinked.

"What is it?" She asked.

"Well, I spent half of the blissies in my pocket on food, and if you spent half of the blissies in your pockets on food, then I don't think we have enough to buy water taxi tickets out of Kazaki." He paused to take a handful of blissies from his pocket. He silently counted the shiny paper blossoms before putting them back in his pocket.

"You're probably right. Still, we don't have much choice," Nia said.

"What if the owner recognizes us and sells us out?" Enjo asked.

Nia considered for a moment. "Then that's a risk that we'll have to take."

"Okay, but then what? What about after we leave Kazaki? It's not like we can just steal the ingredients for the Devastation one by one-"

Enjo took a sip from his drink, and caught Nia's eye. "What?" He asked.

"That's exactly what we're going to do. We steal them one by one, and destroy as much of them as we can. And we don't have a lot of time, either. Seven days from now is when the Paradox plans to use the Devastation, on Eris' day."

"*Seven days?* Why would they be collecting the ingredients now if destroying the world is their ultimate goal? It just feels so... *last minute.*"

"I don't know, but the point is, all we know is that they plan to have all of the ingredients collected and in one place in seven days. How? We don't know."

There was a short pause, then Enjo asked, "But what if we did know? I mean, remember how Namei told us that the Superiors are going to be having a big meeting in the Province of the Water Spirits?"

"No."

"What if we went to the Province of the Water Spirits and listened in on their meeting?"

"Enjo, it'll probably just be the kind of party where spirits laugh politely and tell snobby stories about buying pedigreed unicorns."

At the mention of *pedigreed unicorns,* a gleam came into Enjo's eyes. He'd wanted one for as long as Nia could remember, and the tiny stuffed unicorn he always kept in his pocket was proof.

"But what if it *isn't* and we pass up the chance to get valuable information?" He asked. "What if they already *have* all of the ingredients and they moved them to some other location, just waiting to be taken by us, but we don't know and we go somewhere else and then-"

"Fine Enjo, I get the point. I'd rather go straight for the ingredients and not waste any time, but getting any information we can would be a good choice."

"What were the ingredients for the Devastation again?" Enjo asked.

Nia took the crumpled piece of paper from her pocket. "'A token from Earth, nightclover, the ashes of a Phoenix, the fabric of time, red moon dust, the heart of the mountain, the feather of a Phoenix, and the past, present, and future of Other Side,'" She read aloud. Enjo listened intently. "How many ingredients do you think the Paradox already has?" He asked.

"A token from Earth, definitely. There are things that 'washed up' from Earth all over Other Side." Nia said.

"And nightclover. It's rare and expensive, but I'm sure it's not that hard to get your hands on," Enjo said, twirling his fork in his fingers.

"What about the past, present, and future of Other Side? Any guesses?" Nia asked.

"Probably three of the most historically significant objects in Other Side, but those could be anything."

"And how could the Paradox guess what would be the most historically significant object for the *future* will be?" Nia asked.

Enjo shrugged. "Time travel?" He suggested.

"It all doesn't make sense. It's like the ingredients for the Devastation are more symbolic than they are actual potion ingredients!" Nia said.

"Well, wasn't it the Ancient Spirits who made the Devastation in the first place? They're so powerful, maybe the rules of normal potioneering don't apply to them." Enjo said. Nia waved away his suggestion.

"Maybe. What matters is that we don't know what three of the ingredients *are*, we have no idea how we could get the fabric of time or red moon dust, and we only have seven days before the Paradox plans to use the Devastation!"

"Nia, calm down. Getting stressed won't help anything," Enjo said.

Nia took a deep breath, and exhaled. "You're right. I shouldn't let my emotions control me so easily, it's just-"

"Hard sometimes?" Enjo finished with a smile. Nia nodded, sheepishly. "That's okay," Enjo said, "It's hard for everyone, even if it doesn't seem like it."

"True." She reached into her satchel and took out a map. They pushed their now-empty bowls and cups to the side, and Nia laid out the map. She pointed to Kazaki, in the direct center of it. "Alright, our first stop will be the Province of the Water Spirits, since it's right across the northern side of the moat surrounding Kazaki." She moved her finger up to a huge blue swath on the map. "In the Province of the Water Spirits we'll listen in on their meeting, and if all goes well we'll go west and leave the Province. For now, this is the plan." She moved her finger to the left, tracing their imaginary route. Enjo watched attentively. "We'll go through the Province of the Haffenhafs and the abandoned Province of the Human Spirits, so we can go around the Badlands. Then we'll arrive at the Province of the Fire Spirits and steal the ashes of the last Phoenix, which is one of the irreplaceable items on the list of ingredients." She glanced up at Enjo. His wings had tensed up, and the red feathers on his wings were bristling. *He's thinking about the Province of the Fire Spirits. They hate Harpies there, and Enjo's wings will be a dead giveaway,* She thought. *And if anyone finds out that he's- well, we're dead.* "It'll be fine," Nia said. "We'll go to the Province of the Fire Spirits, steal the ashes, and leave. In and out. Okay?"

Enjo nodded, unsure. She went on, "Then we'll go south to the Province of the Earth Spirits, steal the Heart of the Mountain if its security isn't strong enough to keep out the Paradox or warn the leader of the Earth Spirits, then travel west through the Great Mountains, the Province of the Air Spirits, and the Province of the Harpies to the Province of the Sound Spirits, keeping an ear out for any information on the fabric of time and Paradox activity. In the Province of the Sound Spirits, we'll give the ingredients that we have to Geeta Sebanu-"

"Geeta Sebanu? Wait, why would we give the ingredients to him?"

"He's the safest spirit in Other Side to leave the ashes of the Phoenix and the Heart of the Mountain, way safer than just keeping the ingredients on us. The Paradox is already hunting us down, and having two of the ingredients for the Devastation on us, if we got caught, would be the end of the world; literally."

"But just handing over the ashes of the Phoenix and the Heart of the Mountain to *Geeta Sebanu?*" Enjo asked.

"Why not? He's a friend of our parents, remember?" She paused. "Well, I don't think your dad and him were good friends, but he was close with my parents. And he was in the Assembly as the Sound Spirit Leader, so it's not like he's looking to do the Paradox any favors. And after the ingredients are secured, the Paradox won't be able to make the Devastation."

"And then we'll find our parents?" Enjo asked. Nia rolled up the map, and couldn't hide a smile. "Then we'll find our parents."

They stayed for a few hours more, agreeing it was the only safe place where they could rest. When it was time to set out on their endeavor they pulled their masks and hoods snugly over their faces, and wordlessly the two of them made their way through the crowds to the lower regions of Kazaki, where the cities' criminal underbelly thrived. Nia and Enjo were more acquainted with the darker side of Kazaki than most other spirits their age should have been, and Nia blamed that on the Paradox. They ducked into a back alley, and after pushing aside a few crates they found the stairway they'd taken to Kazaki's lower levels with Namei many times before. The two of them descended the dark staircase and emerged into a large dimly lit area lined with supports that held up the massive buildings above. There were numerous stalls and spirits browsing them, street performers, and cages holding rabid animals Nia didn't recognize. As she stepped off the last step of the staircase she glanced at a wooden sign that always gave her an ominous feeling: "WELCOME TO THE NIGHT MARKET."

On the opposite of the large open area the deck everything rested on opened onto a huge harbor, where dozens of large and run-down boats were moored. Dusk was falling but only a few streetlights were lit, and Nia knew that was intentional.

Nia and Enjo walked through small crowds of suspicious-looking spirits and went straight for a little shack next to a run-down boat. Nia knocked on the door, and a minute later there was a loud crash, then the door burst open and a tiny white dragon spirit came flying out. She spun in the air before gaining her balance, and hovered there before giving Nia and Enjo a once-over. "Ah! Nia! Enjo! I remember you two!" She said, fluttering in the air. Her voice was loud and shrill, typical for someone working in the Night Market.

"Yes, and we heard you started it up again," Nia said, "But we're not here to shut it down. We need tickets out of Kazaki."

"Oh?" The tiny dragon spirit peered at them suspiciously. "And why should I do that? You squirts aren't trying to make a run from the Paradox, are you?"

"Because-" Nia scrambled for an answer, and wished she'd thought that out beforehand. "Because we're on a mission, and we need a trip out of Kazaki."

"Why aren't you with that dragon?" The taxi dragon asked.

"She got discharged, and we got promoted," Enjo said, "And anyway, the Paradox said that if we complete the mission you'd get one-fourteenth of the profits." "One fourteenth-how big would that be?"

Nia and Enjo hesitated. The water taxi dragon scoffed. "Sorry, this isn't some charity ride out of Kazaki! Either pay up or get out!" She said, jabbing her tail at a small sign tacked to the shack. It read: *"Twenty blissies each per trip!"*

"Twenty blissies?" Nia asked. She and Enjo checked their pockets. They had exactly forty blissies each. "Fine, we can pay that," She said.

"Ha, did I say twenty blissies?" The dragon said. "I'm going to raise the price to one hundred seventy blissies, just because you shut down my boat the first time and caused me such a setback. Each!" She cackled. "Now pay up, if you're really that desperate to get out of here. Let me guess, you kids really *are* on the run from the Paradox! Hey, what's you guys' bounty? If it's a high enough price maybe I will give you guys a ride, to the Paradox!" As they spoke the dragon spirit got louder, and suddenly Nia shot out her hand and grabbed the dragon spirit in her fist.

The tiny dragon spirit wriggled and gasped and shrieked. Nia glared down at it.

"We didn't come this far to go back to the Paradox. We *are* using your boat, we *are* getting out of Kazaki, and *you're* going to keep your trap shut whether you like it or not, *got it?*" Enjo and the dragon spirit stared at Nia in surprise. Then the dragon spirit laughed. "It's cute you're trying to intimidate me- hilarious even! But unless you pay up you're not getting across that moat!" She said. Nia wanted to snap at her again, or at least squeeze the little dragon until her eyes popped out like a stress toy. But before she could do either of those things Enjo sighed, and stuffed a hand into his pocket. He pulled out his tiny stuffed unicorn, and held it in his palm. "Would this be enough?" He asked. The dragon slipped out of Nia's grip and quickly flew over, and sat on one of Enjo's fingers. She examined it with an expert eye, muttering aloud as she thought. "White high-quality cloth, invisible stitching... mane and tail in mint condition... are those *pink* diamonds used for the eyes? And a crystal horn? Yeesh, this kid's loaded! You should've offered this to me sooner! Hop on the boat, I'll take you across."

"What? No! Enjo, you can't give that to her!" Nia hissed.

"It's fine, Nia. Really."

"No, it isn't! You've had that your entire life!"

"Are you two squirts finished squabbling yet? Because my boat's either going to the opposite side of the moat or the Paradox, got it?" She snapped.

"Yes, we know. Here's your unicorn," Enjo said. The dragon snatched it in her little claws, looked it over one more time, then flew into a small door built into the shack. A few moments later she flew out again empty-handed. "Great! Now get on the boat you rug rats, I haven't got all night!" She flew over to the boat and flipped a lever, and a piece of board flipped down across a small gap of water, connecting the boat to the dock. Nia and Enjo filed onto the boat, and the waterlogged floorboards creaked and squelched under their weight. The dragon spirit flipped the ramp up again. Then she went to the boat's bridge and flew inside, closing the door behind her. A minute or two later there was a guttural grinding sound that shifted into a loud hum, and the boat began to pull away from the docks. They quickly skimmed through the mass of other boats crowding the harbor and pulled into clearer waters, where only a few fisherspirits' boats lay idly. Nia gripped the boat's handrail and stuck out her tongue to taste the spray. She laughed and glanced at Enjo, beaming. "Isn't this amazing?!" She cried.

The water was growing choppier, and the boat was practically bouncing along the waves now. Enjo was gripping the boat's handrail for dear life, and gave her a queasy smile in reply. She looked out towards the horizon, smiling as the cool wind blew her hair out behind her like a flag. Soon the skyline of Kazaki disappeared behind them, and on all sides of them there was only water. After Enjo had vomited a few times over the side of the boat, they sat down on a wooden bench built into the deck, and Nia patted his back reassuringly. "Feeling better?" She asked. "No. But at least, I don't think there's anything left in my stomach to throw up," Enjo answered, weakly. Behind them the dragon spirit popped out of the bridge, and cackled again. "Well, you better get your sea legs, bird boy! Stop feeding your lunch to the sea!" She said, gleefully. She flew over to them and sat on a wooden perch built into the deck. "Aren't you supposed to be steering the boat?" Nia asked.

The dragon spirit scoffed. "And what, sit there in that box for an hour doing nothing? No, I've got it on autopilot. Nothing to do but sail in a straight line 'til we reach the moat." She spread her wings to embrace the night air, and sighed. "Name's Chilly, by the way. Moon Dragon."

"Nia Angdakila." After a pause she asked, "Wait, you're a Moon Dragon? How did you get here?"

Chilly's eyes lit up with pleasure. "Glad you asked! I was born and raised in the Province of the Moon Spirits. When I was still a dragonet I came to live in Kazaki, the city of promise: where a slice of bread won't set you back fifty blissies, and if you con some sucker out of their lunch money you won't get much more than a slap on the wrist. Only thing I miss about it?" She looked up at the moon, wistfully. "My family stayed behind. I haven't seen them in years." Nia watched the moon's reflection ripple on the water and said, "I haven't seen my family in years, either."

"Really? Where are they?"

Nia didn't answer immediately. She watched a cloud cover the moon, then answered, "I don't know. They were captured by the Paradox years ago, and I haven't seen them since. But I know they're still alive. The Paradox can't touch them."

Chilly scoffed. "No offense, kid, but I wouldn't be so optimistic."

"I'm not about me being optimistic. My grandparents are the Ancient Spirit of Time and the Ancient Spirit of Water. Before I was born they put an enchantment on her so if she was ever hurt, they would know. And unless the Paradox wants Bakunawa and Nisi bent on destroying them, she's untouchable." She said.

Chilly's tiny eyes grew as wide as cherries.

"Hmph! Never thought I'd have a descendant of two of the Ancient Spirits on this rathole."

Then she asked, with a touch of nervousness in her voice, "Want some refreshments or something?"

"No. Although, it would be *great* if you didn't sell us out to the Paradox."

Chilly scoffed again, and folded her front legs indignantly. "And what, miss out on all that coin? Just get as far away from here as you can and you shouldn't have much to-"

There was a sudden lurch as a large wave went under the boat. Chilly was thrown from her perch. She tumbled to the floor and flew up again, sputtering with surprise and anxiety. *"Yeesh! I won't sell you kids out! Sorry!"* She did a nervous figure-eight, then flew down to hover above the waves. *"Hear that, Bakunawa?!"*

The ocean had returned to its calm waves, and didn't respond. Nia laughed, and smiled to herself. *Thanks granddad,* She thought.

It was still dark a few hours later, when land finally appeared over the horizon. As they approached the lights of a harbor and a sprawling town behind it came into view. Nia quickly nudged Enjo with her foot to wake him up, and he looked up from his spot on the deck drowsily. "What? What is it?" He asked.

"Look!" She said, pointing. She stood up from the bench and hurried over to the guardrail, and a few moments later Enjo joined her. A cool breeze carried the smell of tapfruit, dried meat, and other imported goods towards them as they got closer, and Chilly, who'd ducked into the bridge a few minutes ago to steer, guided the boat through the crowded harbor. She steered the boat smoothly into an empty spot and flew out of the bridge. After darting back and forth across the boat tying ropes, tossing down the anchor, and making other preparations she pulled the lever to lower the ramp. It hit the docks with a thud and Chilly said, "Alright, everybody off, I don't have all night!" Nia and Enjo filed off the boat, and as soon as they were off the ramp it was quickly pulled up again, and ten seconds later Chilly's boat tore away from the harbor. Nia and Enjo watched it recede into the distance, then Enjo asked, "You know she's going to tell on us, right?"

Nia sighed, and nodded. Apparently not even the threat of Bakunawa's wrath was enough to deter Chilly from selling them out. "Yep. Let's go."

Nia and Enjo walked through Lanila, where many spirits were up early for Eris' Day preparations, and joined a small crowd for a free shuttle to the Province of the Water Spirits. Neither of them were thrilled to be en route to the Province of the Water Spirits, but the other spirits on the shuttle were. The front half of the shuttle was packed with spirits eager to get their first glimpse at Kasaan, and fortunately, there was plenty of space in the back where Nia and Enjo could sit without being noticed. The doors closed with a *whoosh,* and the shuttle started down the pleasant, willow-lined streets of Lanila. The willows' cyan leaves waved in the early morning breeze and gently stroked the shuttle's windows as they passed. The announcement system of the shuttle said that they'd be arriving in the Province of the Water Spirits in four hours, and soon the two of them dropped off to sleep.

Hours later another announcement signaled they were arriving at their stop, and Nia blearily woke up. She nudged Enjo and he woke up in a daze, and ten minutes later the shuttle came to a stop, the doors opened, and one by one spirits stood up and filed out of the shuttle. As they stepped off the shuttle the excited spirits gasped and snapped photos. Nia and Enjo were the last ones off, and when the bright morning light hit their eyes it dazzled them.

When their eyes adjusted, they gasped. The Province of the Water Spirits was just as beautiful as Nia remembered it. Their stop was built on a pier overlooking Kasaan, the ocean. The sunlight sparkled on the sea, and already Water Spirits from the shuttle were diving into the water, and others were waiting in line for the water jeepney that'd carry them to the areas of Kasaan designed especially for non-Water Spirits. Nia resisted the urge to dive straight into the shimmering water and led Enjo to one of the lines for boats to the Province of the Water Spirits. Fortunately, these boat rides were complimentary too. Nia remembered reading that the Province of the Water Spirits was the richest Province, even richer than the Province of the Moon Spirits, which was known for luxury and wealth. She assumed the free boat rides were to get more spirits into the Province of the Water Spirits, and spend their blissies there.

Nia and Enjo waited in line for a water jeepney, and soon the long line of spirits filed onto the boat. Once everyone was in their seats the boat pushed away from the shore, and the familiar thrill of travel made Nia tremble with excitement. She looked down into the water on the sides of the boat, and gasped. The water was so clear it looked as if the boat was gliding through the air, and beneath the rippling surface she could look down and see hundreds of Water Spirits and other sea creatures darting in and out of undersea buildings, vibrant coral reefs, and kelp forests. Nia couldn't resist the urge any longer. "Enjo, could you hold this for me?"

"Hold what?"

Nia tossed her satchel and book into Enjo's lap, planted her foot on one side of the jeepney, and leaped into the water. The water was cool and fresh, and she sunk into it like it was a soft bed. "Nia?! Nia, are you okay?!" Enjo cried out from the boat. Nia swam up and broke the surface. She beamed up at Enjo, and swam to keep up with the boat. Enjo gave a sigh of relief. "Is the water good?" He asked.

"Yep!" Nia said.

"Why did you just jump in?"

"I'm a Water Spirit! This is water!" She said, playfully splashing water at Enjo. "It's kind of my thing!"

Soon the boat pulled up to one of the "dry" districts of the Province of the Water Spirits. Nia and Enjo looked out in awe at the buildings shining in the sunlight. There were towers carved with swirling designs and all kinds of spirits walking on the platforms that floated on the waves of Kasaan, anchored in place by some strong force. All of the platforms were connected by bridges, and around some of the platforms floating shops drifted in the water.

The water jeepney took them to a dock, and all of the spirits on the boat filed out. This time Enjo was the first one off, and Nia stepped onto the platform beside him.

Nia expected to feel a bigger reaction to coming back to her family's homeland. But she felt strangely detached, like she was just a tourist who'd heard grand things about this place but had no connection to it.

She and Enjo walked away from the line, and after she'd dried herself by using her water magic to pull all the water from her clothes and put it back in the ocean, they grabbed a map from a kiosk. They stood nearby and opened the map, then examined it. "Okay, so where is the meeting taking place?" Nia asked. "Here," Enjo said, pointing to a large building. "It's one of the fanciest restaurants in Kasaan, and it's in one of the dry districts. I don't know much about it, but there might be something in your travel book about it. I'll look at the map and find the best route there." Enjo said. They sat down on a nearby bench, and searched the book and the map intently. Nia quickly found the right page in her book and read, "'Most of the restaurant sits underwater, but above the surface there's multiple towers and a large dome for non-Water Spirit diners. The dome, nicknamed 'the Shell' by locals because the entire restaurant resembles a turtle from above, is extremely expensive to rent and is usually reserved for the Province of the Water Spirit's wealthiest visitors. The dome is charmed with an illusion spell that makes it look like no one's inside, even if someone is, for privacy. There's also a sound magic barrier covering most of the dome,'" Nia read. "How are we supposed to spy on their meeting then?" Enjo asked. Nia studied the image of the restaurant in the book, and said, "I think I have an idea. Let's go."

Enjo led the way to the restaurant. The massive glass dome and matching towers matched the illustrations in the book exactly, and when Nia looked underneath the surface dozens of fashionable spirits were swimming in and out of the restaurant. "So, what now?" Enjo asked. "The book said that the dome was covered with a sound and illusion magic barrier, *but* spells like that can only stretch so far before they get thin and weak. And judging by how huge the dome is and where they'd most want the sound and illusion magic to be strongest," She paused to point triumphantly at the very top of the dome, "That's where the magic is weakest, and that's where we'll spy on the meeting."

Enjo looked up at the dome, and after a long moment said, "Nia, you're brilliant."

"Thank you. Now, what time is the meeting?"

"Namei said eight o'clock exactly."

"Okay, we have a few hours before then. Let's get something to eat and find a hotel, and when night falls, we'll be ready."

Chapter Four
The deceived and their deceiver!

Hours later, they were back on the dome. This time Enjo grabbed her with his feet and flew her to the top. At the very top the surface was flat enough to stand on, so they both crouched down on it and looked through the glass. Below them they could see everything inside the huge dome, which proved Nia's prediction right. She had always assumed there was only a handful of Superiors, but the elegantly-decorated hall was nearly full. All of the Spirits wore cloaks with a white "S" embroidered on the sides of their hoods, and there was a small platform set up near the front of the room. On it, something large was covered with a cloth.

Nia could hear the muffled din of footsteps, jazz music, laughter, and silverware clinking as the Superiors ate from the banquet. Snatches of conversation could be heard from their perch:

"Have you seen those Sand Spirits from the Province of the Earth Spirits? They have curved swords. *Curved. Swords.*"

"Yes, I'll be getting a pedigreed Cuddly from the Province of the Moon Spirits this Harvest Season. From the finest breeder, naturally."

"I heard they're making new investigations into that recent rift in the magical field. Word is, something big is about to happen..."

After a half hour of waiting in silence, Nia fidgeted restlessly. *"They haven't said anything useful!"* She hissed. *"The party isn't over yet!"* Enjo said, defensively. As if on cue, the music stopped and the crowd hushed. The doors to the large room opened, and moments later a spirit dressed in an elaborate grey cloak flanked by two guards stalked into the room. Nia recognized the spirit instantly, and an overwhelming wave of fear and anger crashed over her. Beside her, Enjo gasped. *"The Great Deceiver."*

The Great Deceiver paused, and surveyed the room of Superiors in silence. On his forehead, the black tattoo of the number eight was still there, and for one brief, terrifying moment, the face she'd often seen in her nightmares glanced up at the roof before returning his gaze to the Superiors.

Then he said- in a voice that sounded too average to bear the weight of its owner's infamous reputation- "Hail Eris."

Immediately every voice in the room replied solemnly, "Hail Eris, and may change guide us through the dark." When they were finished the Great Deceiver strode toward the platform. The crowd parted for him and his guards in dead silence. He stepped onto the platform, turned to face the crowd, and cleared his throat. "Superiors of the Paradox," He said, "In six days, the Paradox's vision for a better world will become a reality." He paused, and the crowd hastily applauded. He went on, "Operatives have been dispatched to collect the ingredients of the Devastation. We now have three of the ingredients needed, and we've received word that a fourth one has just been retrieved. One of the ingredients was bought by us at auction only yesterday. 5.8 million blissies is a small price to pay for a better world, isn't it?" There were whoops and cheers of agreement from the crowd. "But what was this ingredient?" The Great Deceiver asked. He smirked and turned to the large object beside him on the platform, covered by a cloth. He pulled away the cloth with a flourish, and underneath it was so dazzling Nia winced and covered her eyes. She quickly looked back, and gasped. It was a mannequin wearing the most gorgeous dress Nia had ever seen or even imagined. Looking at it was a sensation. The fabric was swirling with galaxy nebulas, stardust, shooting stars, and constellations all in one. It was unfathomable, beautiful, and seemed to constantly change as you looked at it. As she moved her head slightly to see it from different angles rainbows of sparkling light could be seen, and although the dress was fashioned as a sort of ball gown, the idea of anyone wearing something so beautiful and unworldly was unthinkable. And the dress had an aura as well: The air around it hung with magic so ancient and vibrant it was overwhelming to sense. The crowd gasped at its beauty, and the Great Deceiver gave a satisfied grin. "Superiors of the Paradox, I give you the fabric of time."

Enjo nudged Nia in the side, and she jumped. "What? What is it?" She asked.

"So what's the plan?"

"Plan- what?"

"The plan to steal the dress! This is a great opportunity!"

Nia looked back at the platform. The dress had been covered again with a large box and two spirits were already wheeling it off the platform towards a door. Her mind raced to think of a plan, and she said, "Enjo, if that box leaves this room it's gone. Forever. We need to break in, *now.*"

"Now?! What about the Great Deceiver?!"

"We don't have a choice! I'm guessing they're taking it to be transported, and if they are it'll be long gone before we can break into that room!"

Enjo's wings trembled, and he gave her a fearful but determined look.

"Alright. What's the plan?"

The box was only a few feet away from the door. The spirits who'd been pushing it fumbled with the keys to the door. Nia glanced at the crowds of Superiors, then the disc of glass in the exact center of the top of the dome. It was huge, thick, and heavy; and most importantly, it looked loose.

"I've got an idea. Quick, help me push this down!" She said. The two of them quickly put all their weight onto the disc of glass. They shoved and pushed until it budged. The jazz music had started up again, but it wasn't enough to hide the scraping of the disc as it was pushed downwards. A few Superiors looked upwards as the disc loosened. The door to the room opened, and the spirits prepared to push the box inside. Nia and Enjo shoved the disc again, groaning and straining.

And after one last push, it fell. It took half a second to clear the drop, and it punched straight through the floor.

There was a sharp crack and a splintering noise as a spiderweb of cracks appeared in the floor. With a sudden lurch it caved in, and every spirit in the meeting hall was dropped into the freezing water of Kasaan, surrounded by shards of glass and fragments of tile.

At once Enjo grabbed onto Nia's shoulders with his feet, and the two of them dropped through the gap. They flew toward the huge box containing the fabric of time and Nia yelled out, "Drop me!"

Enjo dropped her, and she landed on top of it with a thud. The box bobbed under her weight and nearly dipped below the surface. She stood on it in a crouch and took out her daggers, and started to pry the lid of the box open.

The sounds of chaos rang out all around her: Spirits yelling and struggling to swim in the shard-ridden water, alarms blaring throughout the restaurant, and the scramble to rescue all the non-Water Spirit Superiors. Over the confusion someone yelled out, *"She's stealing the fabric of time! Stop her!"* But over the confusion, no one seemed to hear them. Quickly she wriggled her dagger in the small gap between the lid and the box. She jabbed her dagger in further, and wrenched it upwards. The box's lid popped open. Inside was the fabric of time and its mannequin, and Nia quickly started to pull the dress off of it. Then there was a sound that made her blood go cold. The Great Deceiver's voice rang out above the sounds of chaos, more terrifying than the cracking of the glass in the walls, and yelled, *"Stop!"*

Nia's right palm spasmed. She only had moments before the effects of the magic contract set in. She quickly wrenched the dress from its mannequin. There was a tearing sound- and she froze.

And so did everything else.

Chapter Five
A stitch in time!

After a moment, Nia glanced around the room. Splashes of water hung suspended in the air. Enjo, who'd been circling above her, was frozen like an ornament on an infant's mobile. The terrified faces of the Superiors were eerily fixed. Nia stood up on the motionless crate, then looked down at the dress in her hands. The beautiful gown had a small tear near the neck, and Nia gasped. "A tear in time..." She murmured. Then panic started to set in. If fantasy novels had taught her anything, it was that if you messed with time, you regretted it.

Great. I pulled the dress off the mannequin too fast and now time's stopped. How am I even supposed to fix this?! And what's next? Time anomalies? I accidentally fast-forward time to the end of existence? I take us to a timeline where the Paradox has already won? She thought. Nia, hands shaking, carefully folded the dress and put it in her satchel. She looked around again. The room remained as still and silent as a diorama. Nia absently reached into her satchel and touched her travel book. She knew it wouldn't have the answers she needed- not even its obsessive-compulsive authors could have imagined one of their readers would accidentally stop time itself- but its presence was reassuring.

She hummed "In The Hall of the Mountain King" anxiously under her breath, and began scanning the room again. She wasn't sure why, but she felt like she was looking for something.

And then, she spotted them.

A spirit dressed in a Superior's cloak was standing on one of the few unbroken parts of the floor by the doorway to the huge room, hand outstretched towards a spirit in the water like they were trying to rescue them. Their hand was trembling, and the sight sent a chill up Nia's spine. *"Hey!"* She called out, holding her daggers at the ready.

At this the hooded spirit exhaled loudly, and started massaging her arm. "It's about *time* you noticed me." She said. The girl stood up and her oversized cloak fell to the floor, revealing short black hair, a breezy white dress, and bare feet that hovered about three inches off the floor. But despite this, she was still a bit shorter than Nia.

Nia gave a startled gasp. "You're- flying!"

"Yes, I am. And thanks, small spirit!"

Nia blinked, confused.

"I'm sorry, what?"

"For creating this time bubble! Really, you have no *idea* how convenient this is for me." She said. She smirked, and her grey eyes gleamed with satisfaction.

"A- time bubble?"

The girl gave her a blank look before explaining, "It's where a time anomaly can happen safely before it pops, returning the creator of the time anomaly, and the timeline, to its normal course. And even better-" She paused, and clapped her hands twice. An ice cream sundae dripping with chocolate appeared in Nia's hands. "Time is space, and space is time! Anything becomes possible!" The girl said. Nia looked down at her sundae hungrily, but decided not to eat it. Instead, she put it aside and asked, "Who are you?"

The girl gave Nia a surprised look. She glanced at her uniform. "You don't know who I am?"

"No, of course not. How could I?"

After a moment the girl laughed. "You don't need to know my name! I can exist here for a while, since reality here is so... *unstable.*" The girl's eyes gleamed at the word. "But I'm basically a ghost," She said, carelessly. The girl brushed aside her wispy black bangs with a finger and added thoughtfully, "Anyway, this time bubble was something of a lucky break for me- almost like, *destiny!*" She looked around, then Enjo caught her eye. "Who's that?" She asked.

"Him? That's Enjo. We've been friends ever since we were really little." Nia said. The girl's eyes lingered on him, then she looked back to Nia. "Do you still have the fabric of time?" She asked.

"Yes, I have it right here." Nia pulled it halfway out of her satchel, and looked at the small tear around the neck. To her surprise, it was rapidly repairing itself. "Looks like the time bubble is about to pop," the girl said. She used the still-submerged Superiors as "stepping stones" and hovered closer to Nia. She paused, and examined her. Then she said, "You know what, I like you! When you need me, I'll be there- and until then, *I'll be watching you!*"

The girl's cheerful smile shifted into a strange grin, and Nia was hit with an intense smell before the girl disappeared.

Before Nia could react there was a quiet *pop.* And all at once, everything moved.

A rush of sound and movement hit her senses, and she could barely register Enjo's feet grabbing her, and in one swoop, they'd flown through the opening in the dome's ceiling and were flying high above the Province of the Water Spirits.

Nia hung from in his grip, dazed. She was so overwhelmed by what had just happened she couldn't speak, but Enjo was wildly excited. *"I can't believe it! We got one of the ingredients for the Devastation!"* Enjo said, breathlessly. He looked down at Nia, and the excitement on his face was replaced with concern. "Nia? What's wrong, do you feel sick?" He asked. Nia shook her head, ignoring the nauseous feeling growing in her stomach. "I'm fine. Let's just go to the hotel."

When they arrived at the hotel they'd reserved earlier, they went in and approached the front desk. The lobby was dim and drab, and Nia didn't have high hopes for their hotel rooms. A Water Spirit lady with the body of an octopus was sitting behind the desk, asleep. Nia rang the bell on the desk and she jerked awake.

"Here to check in?" She asked, drowsily putting on her half-moon glasses with a tentacle. "Yes, into Rooms 33 and 34. Our names are Nia Angdakila and Enjo Kutana." Nia answered, primly.

The lady flipped through some records, then fetched two keys from a desk drawer and offered them to Nia and Enjo. "Here are your keys. Your rooms are down that hallway and to the left," She said.

They thanked her and accepted their room keys, but as the lady was handing Nia her key she hesitated. Then she gave a fearful glance around the empty lobby and whispered, *"Put something against your door. Lock the door and window. And if you hear sounds from the doorknob, unlock the window and run."*

Nia was so taken back by this, and so overtaken by the events of the day, she didn't ask why immediately. And when her exhausted mind finally thought to ask, the Water Spirit lady had already climbed off her chair and disappeared into the employee break room.

Nia stared blearily at the locked door, then at Enjo. He shrugged. Then the two of them turned and walked down

62

the hallway, looking at the dingy room numbers beside each. The hall smelled faintly of mildew, which wasn't reassuring.

Finally, they got to Rooms 33 and 34. Enjo unlocked the door to room 34 and went inside, then said, "Good night, Nia."

"G'night."

The door to his room closed, and locked. Nia walked into her room, taking care to close and lock it behind her. She surveyed the room. It was small and had nothing but a bed, a nightstand, a small curtained window, and a painting on the wall that looked like someone had dropped a paper bag filled with vomit onto a canvas. But none of that mattered. She collapsed onto the bed and buried her face into the pillows, breathing in the smell of clean linen and another smell she didn't recognize. Her eyelids were so heavy it felt like she'd fall asleep in moments. She lay there, too exhausted to think of the events of that day, and closed her eyes.

Chapter Six
Memories!

Sunlight filled the forest clearing, painting the grass gold and silhouetting the leaves on the trees. Nia watched a flock of birds fly lazily across the sky, then asked, "Hey, dad? How did you save the world before?"

"Well, it wasn't just me. My friends helped."

"But how did you and your friends save the world?"

Nia rested head on her father's side, and felt his breath rise and fall. His scales were cold to the touch, but her father's presence after a long day felt warm and comforting. "And how are you able to turn into a dragon?" She added. Her father smiled, and rested his head on the grass. His long serpentine horns almost glowed in the light of early evening. "That's a long story. But let's just say, they were both hard work."

They were quiet for a while. Then her dad went on, "You know, they say your mother's father- your grandad, Bakunawa- wanted the power of the Devastation for himself."

"Really?" Nia asked, surprised. She'd studied the Devastation with her mother that morning, and the idea of a potion that'd almost destroyed the world with three drops had rattled her.

"Yep. I remember him telling me how he'd succeeded, in tying the power of the Devastation to his own magic- or more accurately, his spirit-magic.

He never did try it out. I guess he thought consuming the Devastation would be too risky."

"Why would he want the power of the Devastation? The Devastation just destroyed things."

"Ah, maybe. But think about it. It'd take a lot of magic to nearly destroy the world, right?"

Nia thought for a moment. "Right," She said. She watched a white butterfly land delicately on a daisy, and balance there. It slowly closed and open it's wings in the mesmerizing way only butterflies can, and Nia hoped it would do it again.

"And that would mean that the Devastation had a lot of magic inside it," Her father continued.

"Right."

"So, if he ever got the power of the Devastation, then your super-powerful granddad would be even *more* super-powerful."

Nia didn't respond. She sat very still, thinking, and looked up at the sky.

"There is one thing he mentioned, though." Her dad added. "If he ever dared to drink the Devastation, he'd be given limitless power."

"Unlimited power?"

A cool breeze blew through the forest clearing, rippling the grass and playing with Nia's hair. *"Wow,"* she said, breathless. "If I had unlimited magic, I'd- I'd- I don't even *know* what I would do."

She met her dad's eye, and he smiled. Then he lifted his head, and Nia sat up.

"Well, we better go. Your mom's probably done with dinner now."

"Do you think she made granola for dessert?"

"Maybe."

He stood up and bent down to let Nia sit between the spikes on his back, and the two of them set off into the sun-drenched woods. Nia loved riding on his back when he was in dragon form, especially on days like today, when he took the path less travelled through the woods. Every time he stepped over a log or climbed up a small hill of dirt Nia would grip onto the spikes on his back and laugh at the sudden change of movement. She held her hand out to touch a wall of flowering bushes as they passed, and asked, "Hey dad? I have a question. No, wait- *lots* of questions."

"I have answers. Hopefully my answers will match your questions," he said, smiling.

"Can we go visit Enjo?"

Enjo and his parents lived in a small town at the end of a winding forest path. His parents and hers were good friends, and from the confidential-sounding conversations they'd have when Nia and Enjo were supposed to be playing outside, they were allies aiding each other in their dream of taking down the Paradox.

"No, not today. We just visited yesterday, remember?"

"Oh, okay. What's spirit-magic?"

"Spirit-magic? It's a very dangerous and powerful magic."

"Mom said I have it."

"Yes, you inherited it from your granddad. It skipped your mother, so you got it instead."

"Is it bad?"

"No, it isn't. But the way you use it can easily become bad."

"What is it, exactly?"

"It's when you can control a spirit and make them do whatever you want, or you can hurt them badly. Apparently it's very painful to endure."

"Well, in that case, I don't think I would ever want to use spirit-magic."

"Good."

After a while Nia asked, "Why does the Paradox not like us?"

"Well, do you remember what me and my friends did after we saved the world?" He asked.

"Yes, you said you all made the Assembly."

"We did. We became spirit-leaders representing each of the eight major provinces of Other Side, and we did our best to make wise decisions. We worked hard to improve the lives of spirits across Other Side, and things went well." He paused to step over a tree stump. "Spirits were happy with us and what we'd done for Other Side, and the peace and prosperity we'd earned seemed like it would last forever. But it didn't."

"So what happened?"

Her father's expression darkened.

"One day the Paradox, a group *no one* had ever heard of before, stormed the hall where me and the other spirit-leaders worked. Their leader was a man who called himself the Great Deceiver, and he demanded us all to give up our positions and come with them quietly. Naturally I laughed at him."

"What did you say next?" Nia asked.

"Don't tell your mom I told you this, but I told him-"

He whispered into Nia's ear, and she raised an eyebrow. After a moment she said, "That doesn't seem like something a leader would normally say, but he deserved it. I'm glad you said it."

"So am I," Her dad said, grinning.

Then his eyes darkened, and he went on. "After that... he attacked us."

"What happened in the end?" Nia asked.

"It ended with six of my friends being captured and taken away. We tried to save them, but we were too late. Me and my friends Rashidi and Sebanu were still unstoppable, but even we couldn't keep up the fight forever. And just when it seemed like we could win, we retreated."

"What? Why?"

At this her dad smiled. "Because your mother sent me a message saying the baby was coming."

Nia's eyes grew wide. *"Me?"*

"Yep. Then I told Rashidi and Sebanu, and three minutes later I was with your mom. And two hours later, you were born."

"Wow," Nia said, "I didn't know *I* would be in this story." Then she asked, "Dad, did Rashidi and Sebanu get captured too?"

"No. When I told them I was leaving they left with me, and we all agreed that as long as our friends remained captured, we wouldn't rest until we found them."

"Have you found them yet?"

Her dad was quiet. Then he replied, "No."

"And did the Paradox say *they* were the new leaders of Other Side?"

"Yes. They did. And they're still the leaders of Other Side, unfortunately."

"Were you hurt in the big fight?"

"Hurt?" Her dad looked at her, jokingly aghast. "Your dad doesn't get *hurt*. I'm invincible, kiddo!"

Nia laughed, and the two of them continued on through the forest.

About ten minutes later, they were home. As Nia and her parents had travelled across Other Side they'd stayed in a variety of different houses, but this one was one of Nia's favorites. It was a small cottage with a green door, and as they got closer Nia could smell the flowers planted around it. She looked around and asked, "Where's mom?"

The house was ominously silent. She couldn't see her mom in the kitchen baking or in the garden reading, where she usually was. Her dad took her to the front door, and she climbed off. When he spoke there was an edge in his voice. "Nia, go inside and lock the door. Stay out of the windows." Nia nodded, and obediently went inside.

"Goodbye, Nia. I love you. I'll be back soon."

"Bye, dad. I love you too."

She closed the door, and locked it. Something inside her hesitated, and she wanted to open the door again and ask him to stay. But she knew better then to argue with her dad when he was worried, so she didn't.

Hours passed. Nia passed the time by drawing flowers in her sketchbook, but every time she peeked out the window in the kitchen the more her parents weren't there. Her mom hadn't made dinner, so she made herself a pot of rice. She was just eating her third helping, and reassuring herself her parents would be back soon, when there was a knock on the door. Knowing better then to open the door for strangers Nia climbed onto a kitchen stool, moved aside a tiny sliver of the kitchen window's curtain, and looked out. Someone she knew was standing on the front porch, but it wasn't her parents. Nia quickly climbed down, went to the front door, and threw it open. *"Enjo? What are you doing here?"* She asked.

He was doubled-over and panting, and his small red wings were limp. When he finally caught his breath he said, *"It's the Paradox! They took our parents! Nia, we need to go!"*

There was the sound of movement far off in the woods, and without warning Enjo grabbed her arm and took off running. Nia glanced back in terror. A pack of gruesome animals burst into the clearing. Their body's were hidden in shadow, but their eyes were like glowing red pinpricks in the darkness. Nia gasped at the sight, and Enjo yelled, *"Nia, watch where you're going!"* She quickly looked back and her knee smashed into a tree stump. Jarring pain ran up her leg. She shrieked and stumbled. Enjo quickly helped her up. Without hesitating they immediately continued running at top speed, and although Nia didn't look back again, the creatures' snarls and bounding footfalls behind them was enough to keep her running for her life.

Their mad dash through the woods was the most nightmarish hour of Nia's life. The trees that were so familiar to her in the day were dark shapes blocking her in. The eternal sound of the pack behind them echoed through the woods. She couldn't think. Terror had consumed her mind entirely. Nothing else in the world existed except her flight from certain death and keeping her footing on the forest floor.

And then, to her horror, something caught her foot. She and Enjo collapsed on the ground and were snatched up by some unknown force, and two seconds later they were suspended ten feet above the ground.

They both sat huddled in the rope trap, paralyzed from shock. Then a moment later Nia shook her head and looked down. The pack of creatures had caught up with them and were circling the ground beneath the trap, growling and snapping. She was about to give a sigh of relief when she heard footsteps in the woods. The cloud that'd been covering the moon drifted away, and moonlight washed over the forest so brightly Nia could see her shadow. A man wearing a hooded cloak stepped into the clearing, and looked up at them with grey, piercing eyes. Nia noticed the black number eight tattooed on his forehead, and shuddered.

"Lower the trap." The man ordered. Instantly it was lowered, and in moments Nia and Enjo were only two feet off the ground. The creatures stood in a circle around the trap, glaring at them but not approaching.

Nia and Enjo looked at the man with huge, frightened eyes. He looked at them for a moment, then asked, "Are you Nia Angdakila and Enjo Kutana?"

Nia and Enjo were too scared to answer. The man did a slow lap around the trap, examining them. Then he paused. He thrust his hand into the trap. Enjo shrieked, and a moment later the man was holding one of Enjo's wings. The man outstretched it and held it with one hand, studying it in the moonlight.

"What color is this, blue? Or-"

The man stopped short. He gave a yell that sent a dozen birds in the distance flying.

Instantly he snatched his hand away from the trap, and looked at it. There were a dozen red marks from where Nia had bit down on it as hard as she could.

There was a shared gasp from the woods, and the man shot back a dangerous scowl.

Then he looked back at the trap, his eyes shining with malice. *"Get these animals out!"* He snarled, massaging his right hand. Two spirits in grey cloaks appeared from the woods and cut open the rope trap. Nia and Enjo fell out onto the ground and were roughly grabbed. "Stand them up," the man ordered. Nia and Enjo were forced to stand in front of him, their arms held behind their backs. The man glared down at them, and terror more intense then their mad dash through the woods grabbed Nia. *What's he going to do to us now? Kill us?*

After a long, torturous moment the man's eyes narrowed. Then he snapped his fingers and said, "Remus."

An ancient, severe-looking spirit glided up from the woods behind him like a shadow. "How may I aid you, Great

Deceiver?" The elderly spirit asked, oily. Nia's eyes grew so wide it felt like they would pop out. *The Great Deceiver! I- I just bit the leader of the Paradox!* She thought. The Great Deceiver asked, "Do you have their contracts ready?"

"Yes, everything except the price of their freedom. I thought I'd leave that up to you."

"Good. I have a fitting price."

'The price of their freedom?' Are they going to let us go? Nia wondered.

The Great Deceiver said dryly, "The price of Nia's freedom will be Enjo's death. The price of Enjo's freedom will be Nia's death."

"Excellent." The elderly spirit disappeared into the woods again.

The Great Deceiver looked down at the two petrified kids, and added, "One more thing."

Then he looked at Nia, and smacked Enjo.

It happened so fast neither of them reacted immediately. Then Enjo's face flushed, and his eye's welled with tears.

Nia's fear vanished immediately and was replaced with rage. "You *monster!*" She snarled. She fought against the spirit holding her back and almost broke free before she was yanked back again. "Take them back to the camp to have their contracts signed," the Great Deceiver said, addressing the spirits restraining them. "Afterwards shave the feathers off his wings and sell them at the Night Market. They'll fetch a good price. And gag the girl." He gave Nia a glare before adding, "The Angdakilas have *foul* mouths."

Nia and Enjo were dragged away into the night, Nia spitting curses she'd never said before and Enjo trying not to burst into tears. They were gagged and blindfolded, and hours later they were forced, hands shaking, to sign the contracts that would bound them to serve the Paradox, and the Great Deceiver, for the rest of their lives.

Later that night Nia and Enjo sat huddled in a small, damp tent in the Paradox camp. The entire tent had been sealed by magic on the outside, so there was no hope of escape no matter how many times Nia tried. Enjo sat at the back of the tent with his head between his knees. He'd wrapped himself in the grey uniform a member of the Paradox had given him like a blanket to hide his bare wings, which looked almost diseased without their feathers. He was sobbing quietly to himself.

Nia, after a futile search for a way to escape, sat next to him. They didn't say anything for a long time, then Nia said, "They won."

Enjo nodded, and continued sobbing.

There was the soft rumble of thunder. Raindrops pattered on the tent's roof. Nia felt herself slip deeper into a swirl of intense despair, and closed her eyes.

Chapter Seven
Water on the sand!

Slowly the vivid memories of Nia's dream faded, and reality started to return to her. Nia blinked, drowsily. Then with a sense of alarm, she realized she was sitting up. She looked around, then she realized she was tied to something. It seemed like she was in some sort of moving tent, because she could see closed flaps fluttering with the movement of the wind and feel movement beneath her.

She did a quick survey of her surroundings. She was sitting against a mast made of wood and sitting on logs wrapped together to make a makeshift raft. She could see sunlight coming in from the slits between the fabrics sewn together, and she could hear a faint *swish,* and see something like dirt being kicked up on the sides of the moving tent. Whatever she was in seemed too crude to be something the Paradox would normally use. *Bounty hunters.* So the Paradox had made a bounty for her at last, and now she'd been hunted down and snatched up by whatever bounty hunter had come to chase her down. She grew sick at the thought, not from fear but disgust. She moved her head and realized she was gagged, then looked at her arms. Unfortunately, she'd been asleep- or knocked out by some chemical or poison, most likely, which must've been that strange smell she hadn't recognized last night- when her captors had gotten her, or she would've taken a deep breath before she was tied up and exhaled when her captors had left, loosening the rope. It was a technique Namei had taught her.

She could see that the rope was a rough one, and if she struggled from it too much her arms would get scratched. So she decided to make every movement count. After taking inventory of what she had- fortunately, she'd been so exhausted last night she hadn't taken off her satchel or water bottle, and neither of those things had been confiscated- she reached into her pocket and felt for her ring. Fortunately, it was there. It was an iron ring that looked normal when she wore it, except that the part facing her palm had a razor edge. She put it on carefully to avoid touching the sharp part and moved her hand toward her rope. Then she rubbed the sharp edge of the ring on the rope and it began to sever through it. After ten minutes of sawing through the rope the last threads of the first rope binding her were cut through. She started to cut through the next rope and five minutes later, the rope split, and the second rope was cut. As she did she kept an ear out for any shifts in her surroundings, but there were none. She knew she had to keep cutting through the ropes and break free before this moving raft stopped, but as she was sawing through the third rope there was a whistle from outside and the raft came to a sudden stop. She quickly turned her ring around so that the sharp part was facing her palm, then slumped her head and closed her eyes just before the flap of the tent flipped open. Nia sensed a spirit hesitating in the doorway and tensed. The spirit stood there for a moment, then Nia heard the unsheathing of a knife. The spirit advanced towards her. Nia's heart began to race with anticipation. Did the Paradox ask for her to be brought to them dead or alive in her bounty description? Nia couldn't bear the suspense any longer. She could imagine the bounty hunter wondering which way to kill her, and which way would obscure her features the least so the Paradox would recognize her when it was time to collect the bounty. She braced herself to break out of the ropes and attack, and she sensed the knife beginning to grow closer to her.

Suddenly the knife hacked through the rope in one move, and Nia opened her eyes in surprise. She caught a glimpse of a slim girl wearing simple desert attire. The girl was about her age, with dark brown skin, curly black hair, and golden dust that shimmered on her cheeks. She grabbed Nia's hand and suddenly she was jerked to her feet.

"Come on, I'm rescuing you!"

There was a sudden blast from outside, and the raft they were on shook. Nia nearly lost her balance, but the girl kept her steady. "Let's go!" She said. Nia didn't argue. The two of them ran from the tent into the open, and as Nia's eyes met her surroundings she gasped. It was the complete opposite of what she'd seen yesterday in the Province of the Water Spirits. Around her on all sides stretched an endless expanse of sand, but immediately in front of her, she saw a kayak with boards on either side of it for balance. Nia slowed, but at the sound of another explosion she picked up the pace. Her bare feet sunk deep into the blistering sand, but the girl who'd rescued her was deftly darting on the sand's surface. "Don't slow down, keep up with me!" The girl said. She sped ahead of Nia and jumped onto the canoe, and Nia, confused but deciding this wasn't the time to argue, jumped into the seat in front of her. As she did she could see a long caravan of boats on the sand behind them, and one of them was tied to the raft she'd been trapped on. Dozens of spirits were evacuating the boats, trying to extinguish flames that were quickly devouring the head ship. Suddenly the canoe beneath her began to shift direction, then the small ship turned and began to glide across the sand at high speed. Nia hastily pulled up the mask of her uniform and gripped the sides of the boat. She could see nothing but the endless stretch of sand in front of her, and when she glanced behind them she could see two ships peel away from the rest and chase after them. Sand hit Nia's face as the canoe raced along the sand. "How is this boat *moving?!*" Nia shrieked. "My Earth Magic! I'm pretty talented, as you no doubt noticed!" The girl called back, forced to raise her voice over the wind. Nia looked back, and saw the girl standing above her like a gondolier

79

on a small plank, holding onto a rudder. Something whizzed past them and exploded in a burst of color and heat, then the entire canoe shifted and was pushed on the shockwave. "What was that?" Nia yelled. The girl had quickly regained course, but more of the bombs were raining toward them. "A problem! But don't worry, we can outrun them!" She answered back. Their canoe sped on, and carried them through the desert. Soon the caravan was nothing more than a plume of smoke, far away in the desert behind them.

An hour later the sand of the great desert receded and made way for dirt and rock, and a huge mountain pierced the horizon in front of their skiff. The late morning sun rose above the mountain and dazzled Nia's eyes, and when her eyes adjusted she saw they were rapidly approaching a huge city. Spiraling stone towers stood over smaller buildings made of earth and rock, and the hundreds of streets were crowded and lively. As they came closer the girl who'd rescued her gave a happy sigh. "Welcome to the Province of the Earth Spirits!" She said. She guided their boat to an elaborate tower, and after "mooring" the skiff nearby, beckoned Nia to follow her. She pushed open a heavy wooden door and led her inside. They climbed a spiral staircase and walked out onto the top floor. It was completely open to the outside, and instead of stone Nia realized she'd stepped onto soft grass. The entire top floor was a beautiful garden with blossoming flowers and fruit bushes, and in the center of the magnificent garden was a set of table and chairs. But it wasn't the garden's beauty Nia noticed first. It was the table and chairs arranged at its center and the two spirits seated there: Enjo, and a tall man dressed in traditional armor who looked like he could've been her rescuer's father. They were having a heated argument, and they didn't stop as Nia and the girl walked in.

"Why can't I go after them?" Enjo asked.

"If you went out there again alone, you'd be finished."

"I can't just sit here and do *nothing* while my friend's out there!"

"I won't allow you to go after her, so you don't have a choice. There's no Harpy alive that could withstand the heat of the Great Desert for long." The man said. Enjo's eyes flashed with annoyance, but he was quiet. The man opened his mouth to speak again, but stopped when he noticed Nia and her rescuer. "Ryoko!" "Dad!"

The girl hurried over and gave the man a warm hug. Then she let go and said excitedly, "The rescue went great!"

"Excellent! Nia, Ryoko, have a seat," The man said. The two girls took the remaining seats at the table. Immediately Enjo asked, "Nia! Are you hurt? What happened?"

Before Nia could say anything Ryoko said proudly, "She'd been captured by the Sand Spirits. After I found them I snuck onboard, wrecked the engine of the main boat, and rescued her. Then we got in my boat and escaped the Sand Spirits chasing us."

"Very good, Ryoko," The man said. "Before we go on, I think we should introduce ourselves. Nia, I'm Rashidi, the Premier of the Earth Spirits. This is my daughter, Ryoko."

Nia's eyes lit up with recognition. "Rashidi- you were the Earth Spirit Leader!"

His eyes darkened, and he cleared his throat uncomfortably. "Yes, I was." Then he asked, "Nia, how did you end up being captured by the Sand Spirits?"

"I don't know. I fell asleep in a hotel in the Province of the Water Spirits and woke up trapped on one of their boats. Enjo- wait, you were in the room right next to mine. What happened?"

Nia looked to Enjo expectantly, and all eyes were on him. When he realized everyone was staring at him Enjo's face flushed.

He stammered, and after he paused to collect his thoughts he said quickly, "I woke up in the middle of the night when I heard a weird sound coming from Nia's door. I thought she was just getting up to use the bathroom or something, so I went back to sleep. Then a while later I got this weird feeling that I should go check, so I got up. The door to Nia's room was open and she was gone."

"So I got kidnapped because you were too tired to get up and check on me before?"

"I flew you back to the hotel, remember?! I was exhausted!" Enjo said, defensively. Nia shot him a glare.

"Enjo, please continue," Rashidi said.

"Well, after that I ran out of the hotel, and I saw two spirits dragging Nia into a building across the street. I ran after them and burst into the building, but as soon as I did I got sucked into a- what's it called again?" He asked, addressing Rashidi.

"A spirit-circle. The fastest way of getting across Other Side that there is."

"Right. As soon as I stepped inside I was pulled into a spirit-circle, and the next thing I know I was dropped in a huge sandstorm. I couldn't see or hear anything, so I had to take shelter under a dune of sand. Then Ryoko found me and brought me back to the Province of the Earth Spirits. I told Rashidi what happened, and he sent Ryoko to go and rescue you," Enjo said.

"But the Sand Spirits are just thieves and bounty hunters. They wouldn't go after someone unless they had a huge bounty on their head, so why would they-?" Ryoko asked. She paused and looked at the two of them suspiciously, eyeing their Paradox uniforms. Nia and Enjo exchanged glances, and Nia sighed. "Yes, I probably have a huge bounty on my head. We're on the run from the Paradox."

"I knew it!" Ryoko said.

"On the run from them? How did you get to be working for them in the first place?" Rashidi asked.

"It's a long story," Enjo said.

Nia explained quickly, "Our parents were captured by the Paradox, and the Paradox forced us to work for them. We aren't sure why, but we've been working for them and trying to escape for three years. We finally escaped three days ago, and we have information about the Paradox's ultimate goal."

At this Rashidi leaned forward some in his chair. His brow was drawn together with visible concern. "And what is their 'ultimate goal?'" He asked.

"In four days they plan to recreate the Devastation, and use it to kill every spirit in Other Side."

There was a brief silence as Nia and Enjo waited for Ryoko and Rashidi to digest what Nia had told them.

"Where did you learn this?" Rashidi asked.

"From this," Nia said. She took the crumpled piece of paper from her pocket, and handed it to Rashidi. He and Ryoko read it in silence, then Ryoko gasped. A new look of seriousness came over Rashidi. "There's no doubt. It's in the Great Deceiver's handwriting," He said. "Nia, Enjo, what were you two doing in the Province of the Water Spirits?"

Enjo looked to Nia as if to ask, *Should we tell him?*

Nia nodded and said, addressing Rashidi and Ryoko, "We were in the Province of the Water Spirits to learn more about the Paradox's plans to recreate the Devastation, and we left with the fabric of time. The Great Deceiver had it on display for the Paradox's Superiors, and we stole it. Enjo and I's plan was to steal the ingredients of the Devastation, one by one."

"And what ingredient were you planning to steal next?" Rashidi asked.

"The ashes of the phoenix."

Ryoko's eyes went wide. "You can't just *steal the ashes of the Phoenix!* Do you have any idea how important that is to the Fire Spirits?" She asked. Her hands were gripped so tightly around the table's edge it looked like it would snap at any moment.

"Ryoko." Rashidi gave his daughter a stern glance. "Let them go on. Nia, Enjo, I can't say that I encourage you two to steal our ally's most treasured artifact- my position won't allow me- but I will say this."

Everyone seated at the table paused at the sudden whiff of wildflowers, and a dozen envelopes fell onto the table in front of Rashidi. He glanced over them dismissively. "Are they more letters about the preparations for Eris' Day?" Ryoko asked.

"Yes, I'll deal with them later," Rashidi said. As he went on he kept his expression and voice stern and poised, but he couldn't hide the strained traumatic look in his eyes.

"I was much younger when the Devastation was unleashed. I wasn't there to see the Ancient Spirits use the three drops upon the Province of the Giant Spirits, but I felt its effects. And so did everyspirit in Other Side. In seconds it consumed almost everything, leaving nothing but ash. Only a few places in Other Side were left untouched, and that was where the only spirits survived. I was lucky enough to be in the Great Desert at the time," Here he paused to close his eyes, and grimace. "It didn't take long for the surviving spirit's worlds to be flipped upside down. Resources became almost nonexistent. Survival became everyspirit's only goal, and the things they did to achieve it was unspeakable. Wanting to help the other spirits of what was left of the Province of the Earth Spirits peacefully, I traveled across what we called the 'Wastelands,' searching for anything salvageable and bringing it back to the survivors in the Great Desert. During that time, I met Gakusei and Sebanu."

Nia's eyes blazed with silent satisfaction at her father's name, and she sat up a little straighter in her seat.

"Gakusei was crazy- he actually believed he could reverse the effects of the Devastation, all because of some ancient relic. I decided to go with him, and that turned out to be one of the best decisions of my life. It turns out he'd been right about that relic, and with the help of some friends we met along the way and the Ancient Spirit of Time, we were able to reverse the effects of the Devastation on Other Side, for the most part. The one part we couldn't save, the former Province of the Giant Spirits, became the Badlands; all that's left of the Decay. Nia, Enjo- the Paradox *must* be stopped, or else this world, and everyone in it, will die."

"Then we can't waste any more time. Enjo, we're leaving." Nia said. She and Enjo stood up from their seats.

"Before you leave, I think it'd be wise if I assigned someone to guide you to the Province of the Fire Spirits," Rashidi said.

Nia blinked. "What? No, we're fine-"

"I won't take no for an answer. Ryoko, go straight to Amba and give her the details. Tell her to guide Nia and Enjo safely to the Province of the Fire Spirits and help them retrieve the remaining ingredients of the Devastation."

Ryoko scowled. "I can't. She's out on that big raid on the Sand Spirits, remember?"

"Alright, then I'll assign Seth."

"Seth died last week. He got caught up in that skirmish between the Fire Spirits and the Harpies outside the Gateway."

"Really? How inconvenient. Brent will do, then."

"No, he was showing some tourists the Edge of the World when he got reckless and pretended to step off the side. He slipped and fell, and the tourists say they're pretty sure he's still falling."

"Rita?"

"Got bit by a Chomper last week."

"Wren?"

"He couldn't guide someone out of a paper bag."

Rashidi sighed, and pinched the bridge of his nose. "Ryoko, is there *anyone* available who could help these two?" He asked.

Ryoko's eyes lit up. A grin crept up her face, and she was failing miserably at hiding it.

"Well, there is *someone…*"

Rashidi gave his daughter a sharp look. "Ryoko, I can't send you on this assignment. It's far too dangerous, and it'd take you outside of the Province."

"But it'd give me a chance to take back the Heart of the Mountain!"

"Wait, was it stolen?" Enjo asked.

"Yes, only yesterday. Dad, I can handle myself! Out of all the guides in the Province of the Earth Spirits, no one's more prepared than me! Please?" Ryoko pleaded. Her father sighed.

"You can go."

"*Yes!*" Ryoko pumped a fist in the air. "And I'll be back with the Heart of the Mountain!"

"I'm more concerned about your safety, Ryoko. Don't even *think* about getting lost or hurt."

"I'm the best adventurer in Other Side! I'll be fine."

"Good."

After they exchanged goodbyes with Rashidi, Ryoko took them to a storage building. It was a small, square building lined with shelves and crammed with clay pots, sewn parcels, and spicy desert herbs drying upside down from the ceiling.

Nia and Enjo were free to gather what they pleased. She picked out a sturdy, modern water bottle to replace her old one and gathered medical supplies, packaged food, and water while Enjo packed other "necessities," which included a large bag of unicorn-milk chocolate bars. She watched him aggressively squeeze it into the top of his bag and asked, "You know you're going to have to carry all that, right?"

"I know, but it'll be *so* worth it."

After packing their supplies and everything they would need on their journey, Ryoko took them to the border of the Province of the Earth Spirits. In front of them tall mountains nearly touched the sky, and Nia stared up at them in wonder. They all wore backpacks, and Ryoko had given Nia and Enjo traveling clothes to wear. It'd been bliss for Nia to finally be rid of her Paradox uniform, and she and Enjo had burned them shortly afterward. Now as she looked up at the mountains ahead of them, she almost wished they'd kept them. It looked like they'd need as much campfire fuel that they could get their hands on.

She looked to Ryoko, who had her arms crossed and was looking up at the mountains thoughtfully. Enjo asked nervously, "How are we going to get across? Are we going to have to climb?"

Ryoko thought for a moment, then said, "Yes, we're going to have to climb. Neither of you have lung problems, right?"

Enjo's wings went limp. Nia stared at the mountains, which suddenly seemed even taller and unclimbable than they had a moment ago. Ryoko burst out laughing. "Of *course* we're not going to climb! We'll go through the Gateway. It's a place between the mountains that's flat and easy to cross through. Follow me."

A few minutes of walking later, the sides of the mountains dropped abruptly to form a hallway-like pass through the mountains. It was long and cut right through the mountains to the other side, and hundreds of spirits were walking through with carts and farm animals. It was almost too good to be true.

Enjo gave a sigh of relief. Nia looked at the Gateway with relief, then suspicion.

"Is there a toll?" She asked Ryoko.

"No."

"Guards?"

"Yes, but we don't need to worry about them. We're not the ones they're looking for."

"Mountain monsters that kill anyone who comes through the pass?"

"Ask them," Ryoko said, jerking her head to the spirits walking through. Nia bit her lip. Things were never this easy.

"You have a point. Maybe I'm just paranoid," She said. Nia squinted at the Gateway, then followed Ryoko as she led the way into it.

Carved into the rock, presumably by Earth Magic, were buildings. Most of them were shops catering to tourists and other spirits going in and out of the Gateway. There were staircases and balconies carved into the rock, and the Gateway was teeming with life. It reminded her of a street in Kazaki, but everything was bursting with the distinctive style of the Province of the Earth Spirits. Plants and vines were growing out of the rock and hanging down the sides of the mountain pass. Nia smelled one with purple flowers as she went, and sighed at the sweet smell. Above her beautiful multi-colored cloths stretched between buildings fluttered in the breeze.

They followed Ryoko through the Gateway, and even though Nia felt like she'd never run out of things to look at, the walk was slow. "How long is it until we're out of the Gateway?" She asked. "Two minutes. Unless we walk." Ryoko answered, turning suddenly. She led them down a narrow alleyway that sliced straight through the rock, and as Nia followed Ryoko her shoulders brushed against the side of the course rock. The dim alley was lit only by lights placed on shelves carved into the walls, and the alley was made darker by the fact that there was no sky above. They were surrounded by stone on all sides, and as they walked further down it slowly became unbearable. Nia tried to reach up to wipe the sweat from her forehead, but there wasn't enough room to move her arm. She was about to open her mouth to ask how Enjo and Ryoko could stand it when Ryoko asked, "Isn't this great? Being *surrounded* by dirt and rock?"

"No," Enjo said, thoughtfully. "But I bet if I was an Earth Spirit like you, I'd be enjoying it more."

Nia choked back the claustrophobic remark on her tongue.

"Where exactly are we going?" She asked. Ryoko patted one wall and said dreamily, "I bet this is what swimming is like for a Water Spirit. It feels good, being surrounded by your own element." She took in a deep breath, and let out a contented sigh. "But as for where we're going," Ryoko continued, "We're going to a spirit-circle. There's a handful of public access spirit-circles in the Center, but none of them take you straight to the Province of the Fire Spirits."

"Because they're at war," Enjo said.

"Exactly, it would be a huge safety hazard. But unbeknownst to the public, my dad had one installed for elite ambassadors to the Province of the Fire Spirits."

She went quiet, and glanced back at Nia and Enjo before looking away again. There was an uneasy look in her eye, and Nia immediately noticed it.

"So you're saying we can teleport straight there if we use this spirit-circle?" Nia asked. There was an edge in her voice, and she hoped Ryoko wouldn't notice it. "Well, yes," Ryoko answered. "The thing is, it's kind of...finicky? Sometimes it takes spirits to the Province of the Fire Spirits, and sometimes it doesn't."

"Where do the spirits end up when it doesn't?" Enjo asked. His left-wing twitched nervously.

"You don't want to know," Ryoko said.

"Isn't there some other way to get to the Province of the Fire Spirits?" Nia asked.

"I wish there was. But unfortunately, we don't have a choice. When we go in, just don't freak out, okay?"

They were finally nearing the end of the tunnel-like alleyway, and as they grew closer Nia looked over Ryoko's shoulder at a metal door that ended the tunnel. Ryoko did a complicated series of rhythmic taps and knocks upon its surface, and suddenly the door melted away into thin grey smoke, revealing an open doorway and a passage beyond it.

Ryoko looked back at Nia and Enjo, and smiled triumphantly. She led them through the doorway, and Nia and Enjo exchanged glances before following. The passageway opened up into a spacious hall with no other rooms branching off of it. What immediately caught Nia's attention was that the room was empty. She turned to ask Ryoko if there'd been some mistake, but paused. Ryoko closed the door and locked it. Nia's stomach suddenly lurched. She screamed out of instinct and felt herself being plucked backward as a massive surge of magic burst from the center of the room, and she fell headfirst into the most overwhelming magical experience she'd ever had. She couldn't see anything except occasional flashes of light, but she could feel everything. Disembodied hands of magic crawled up her limbs, tickling her nervous system and making her flinch from the sensation. The familiar electrifying feeling she got from water's touch was there as well, but instead of lighting her up inside it felt like a live wire was thrashing inside her, sparking wildly. She was still falling, and suddenly she froze in mid-air. The strange flashes of light slowly grew brighter until she could see again. She saw a light grey expanse slowly change from white to a dull grey, like it was white paper absorbing grey paint. And as the white expanse turned to grey she hung in the air, suspended, and braced herself to fall.

Chapter Eight
Above and beyond!

The three of them were sent spinning in space, and Nia was flipped over and over in emptiness. It was too quick to register anything except shock, dizziness, and the speed of her falling from the sky. All thoughts stopped. She could only remember that she'd felt like this before, once in a nightmare. She felt terrified, but she didn't have time to scream. Moments later she glimpsed something dark and barren underneath her, then she slammed into a pile of ash that knocked the wind out of her. She lay there, shaking. To her, the world was still spinning. A few moments later, Enjo spiraled out of the sky and landed in a heap ten feet away, then Ryoko gave an unceremonious landing a few feet away from Enjo. She bounced on impact and rolled to a stop, her curly black hair covered in ash and dirt. Enjo was shaking all over, and none of them made a sound except for Nia and Enjo gasping for air.

Then Nia sat up and ran her fingers through her hair, hoping to get all the dust and dirt out of it. She failed, and looked to Enjo. He'd sat up as well and was huddled beside Ryoko, still shaking. She looked at Ryoko. She hadn't moved.

"Ryoko!" She scrambled over and sat beside her. She rolled her upright. Her eyes were closed, and she'd cut her foot on a rock. At once Nia pulled off her pack, which was fortunately still securely on her back, and grabbed her medical supplies. She cleaned and bandaged Ryoko's foot, then checked Ryoko's head for any signs of concussion.

Enjo had taken off his pack, and when Nia looked back at him, certain that Ryoko hadn't had a head injury, Enjo was stuffing his face with chocolate. *"Enjo! That was for emergencies!"* She snapped.

"I'm stressed! And hungry! I can't help myself!" Enjo said, as the last chunks of rich chocolate disappeared in his mouth. He savagely licked his fingers, then added, "And this *is* an emergency."

Nia groaned, then turned her attention back to Ryoko. Her eyes were closed, but her heart was still beating normally and there was no sign of her having a serious head injury-except the knock on her head she'd no doubt received when she hit the ground so awkwardly. Nia was digging through the pack for something else that might help when a sound brought her attention back to her surroundings. It wasn't the kind of sound that was easy to describe. It was like a rumble in the distance, only more subtle, like a shift in the presence of everything she felt around her. It reminded her of a sound she'd learned while she'd been working for the Paradox in Kazaki, when a dragon taxi was flying in the distance. Her instinct, honed by years of training under Namei and the stress of missions, brought the sound to her attention immediately. She looked around. There was no one except Ryoko and Enjo, who was now getting unsteadily to his feet. When she looked past him, the severity of their surroundings hit her like a stone. The land all around them was barren and the color of ash. Nia stood up, and reached for her daggers.

Suddenly the ground opened, and something burst out to lash out at Nia. In an instant, Nia grabbed a dagger from its sheath on her belt and blocked something as it flew towards her. The thing wrapped around her dagger and nearly jerked it back towards it, but Nia slid her dagger from its grip and jumped back. The thing retreated into the ground, leaving a gaping hole exposed. *"Enjo! Fire in the hole!"* Nia barked.

Enjo scrambled over to the hole and took in a deep breath, then blew. Fire erupted from his mouth and burst into the hole, and there was a terrible screeching sound as the stench of charring flesh flew from the hole. Enjo held his arm up to his face to shield himself from the heat. Nia came nearer, and as she did an intense smell rose to meet her. She gagged, and came close to Enjo's side. Nia looked into the hole. Inside was the body of a monster that was being ravaged by flames. The monster wriggled and lashed its mutated limbs in the air, running into the sides of the hole uncontrollably. The stench was frightful.

Nia grimaced at the sight.

"What is *that?*" Enjo asked.

"A mutant. And that means-"

But before she could answer the monster vaulted itself out of the hole. The monstrous beast hung in the air, poised to land on Nia and Enjo, and in that split second Nia braced for impact. Then there was the sound of a blow landing, a horrible screech, and something wet landed on Nia's face. She opened her eyes in shock, and the monster was gone. Its remains were splattered all around them.

Beside her, Enjo coughed up something brown. "Ugh- monster gunk!" He said, gagging. Beside them Ryoko was standing beside them covered with blood. She hastily wiped her face on the back of her sleeve before looking at them, confused.

"What?" She asked.

Nia and Enjo stared back at her in shock.

"What just- *happened?*" Nia asked.

"I punched it," Ryoko answered, simply. She toed a monster part with her foot. "Still, my technique needs work. Some Gatekeepers could've disintegrated this thing if they wanted to."

"*Gatekeepers?*" Enjo asked.

"Talented spirits who maintain the peace of the Province of the Earth Spirits- basically professional adventurers. I'll be one someday, but for now, I need to guide you two to the Province of the Fire Spirits. Now, we're in the Badlands. And if we're in the Badlands, that means something went wrong with the spirit-circle. It also means that we're closer to the Province of the Fire Spirits than we were before." Ryoko said. The cheerful and outgoing side of her they'd seen in the comfort of the Province of the Earth Spirits had been replaced with grave seriousness, and she seemed completely focused on escorting Nia and Enjo safely. She took out a map from her backpack. On the map were three names: **Nia Otohime Angdakila, Enjo Kutana**, and **Ryoko Bayani.** The names hovered above the Badlands, a dark scar on the map. And according to the map, they were extremely close to the Province of the Fire Spirits. Nia studied the map with Enjo, then Ryoko rolled it up. She took out a compass, and after a moment put it away again. She stood up, and pointed west. "Alright, that's the way we need to go. Are you two ready?" She asked. "Lead the way," Nia said. The three of them set off west for the Province of the Fire Spirits.

Hours later, the cracked ground of the Badlands still stretched around them in all directions. Besides the occasional gnarled tree or rotting corpse of a monster, they'd seen nothing besides dirt and ash. The stench of the burning monster seemed to follow them on the wind, and Nia was glad the tunic she wore had a bit of fabric that she could pull over her nose and mouth to serve as a mask to block out the smell. The heat was unbearable. Sweat made her face and neck slick, and the front of her tunic was soaked. The sun was scarlet and glaring. Even Enjo, who Nia knew had extreme resistance to heat, was beginning to flag. Ryoko suddenly dropped onto her knees, and panted. Nia and Enjo paused behind her. "Maybe I- pushed us too much." She panted. "Let's take a break here."

Enjo nodded, and he and Nia collapsed onto the ground. They lay there, panting, and Ryoko took out their water bottles. First she handed Enjo his water, and he sucked it down graciously. Then she handed Nia hers. Nia thanked her and drank. The water felt cooler and sweeter than the water she drank in Kazaki, and Nia knew because now, it was more precious. She gulped it down, then wiped a drop of water off her lips with the back of her sleeve. She felt refreshed, even though the heat continued to cascade on her, grabbing her with suffocating hands and making her wet with sweat. She and Enjo both sat up. Ryoko sat down next to them and chugged down her own water before putting it away. Nia wiped off her face, but it quickly grew wet again. Now that he was refreshed, Enjo seemed back to normal now. In fact, he was even cheerful. "Nia, what do you think the Province of Fire Spirits is like?" He asked. "My dad said it's really strict in the army and towards foreigners, but when you live there, it's not that bad. They play games in the streets all the time, and most spirits are friendly. I wonder what we should eat there! And-" He paused, and his eyes lit up. "Nia, could I have your book?" He asked.

Nia nodded, and handed him her book.

Enjo started to flip through it, but he'd hardly started reading before Ryoko snatched it away.

"Hey!"

"Look, Enzo-"

"My name is Enjo."

"Look, you're sitting right next to a soon-to-be legendary Gatekeeper. Ask *me* questions about the Province of the Fire Spirits! I'm your guide!"

"Thanks, but I'd rather look in the book."

Ryoko looked offended. *"Why?"* She asked.

Enjo didn't answer. Nia sighed.

"He likes looking at the pictures of unicorns, but he feels like that would be a childish response so he doesn't want to tell the truth. Talking about the Province of the Fire Spirits probably reminded him of that special breed of unicorn he's always going on about," Nia said.

Enjo's face flushed.

"Unicorns?" Ryoko asked. An amused smile crept up her face, and she snickered before standing up. "You two are kind of crazy, aren't you? Come on, we have to keep going. We don't have a moment to lose."

One hour later, they arrived. It was late afternoon, and Nia was pleased they hadn't lost much time. The closer they approached the Province of the Fire Spirits the closer they got to the huge wall that encircled the entire province. Nia expected it to be made of brick, but as she got closer she gasped- the entire thing was made out of magma. As she got closer a wave of heat washed over her. The wall was dark with glowing cracks of yellow and red lava, and even though it was made from magma, Nia was astonished to see that it was badly damaged in places.

The three of them approached the main gate set into the wall of lava, and gasped. The entire area around the wall was covered in serious battle scars. The ground around the wall was scarred with deep gashes and other marks of impact. All around the wall Fire Spirits were hurrying with wagons full of lava bricks and magma in buckets for mortar. Other Fire Spirits were hurrying around with sacks and scattering the contents, seeds and sometimes whole plants, onto the ground in front of the wall. No one stopped them as Nia, Enjo, and Ryoko came up to the main gate, but as they passed Nia noticed at least a dozen Fire Spirits give Enjo bewildered glances. She couldn't blame them. Nia doubted anyone who even *looked* like a Harpy had managed to get this close to the wall in years; at least, no one with peaceful intentions, like Enjo. Nia realized that it'd probably been the Harpy army who'd damaged the wall so badly, and she wondered how the Fire Spirits would react if they knew the truth about Enjo. *Maybe they'd have sympathy for him, since-?* She quickly dismissed that thought. She knew exactly what would happen if spirits knew the truth, and the thought made her grimace.

101

The three of them walked up to the main gate. There was a Fire Spirit on the wall above, and she called out, "Who are you?"

Nia looked up. Before she could respond Ryoko stepped in front of her and said, "My name is Ryoko Bayani. I'm here on my father Rashidi's orders, escorting two spirits under the protection of the Province of the Earth Spirits. Their names are Nia Angdakila and Enjo Kutana. Why we're here is confidential, but I have my father's seal to prove our authenticity." She took a violet jewel engraved with a seal out of her pocket, and showed it to the guard.

The guard scrutinized it for a moment, then her eyes went wide. She turned to another guard and whispered something, and the two of them had a fierce discussion before the first guard turned back to the three of them. "You have clearance. Take these."

The guard tossed down cards with their names hastily written on them. These "clearance cards" said that they'd been given permission to come in, why they were let in, and their names. Nia looked down at her card, and scowled at the words "Helpless child." As she put away her card she caught a glimpse of Enjo's. It was printed in a language- or some kind of code- she didn't recognize, but she didn't think about it much.

The guard who'd thrown down their cards went around the wall barking orders, and a few moments later the main gates swung open, revealing the Main Street of the Province of the Fire Spirits, paved with dark red bricks and lined with statues of past Fire Spirit warriors. The three of them moved to go in, but the guard called out, "Stop! The Harpy goes in first!"

"Why?" Ryoko asked.

"Don't know, but it's a direct order from Great House Amaterasu. Either you play by their rules or hit the road. Your choice."

The three of them exchanged glances. Then Enjo smiled weakly. "It's fine. I'll go first."

He took a step forward, but Nia held him back. Alarm bells were ringing in her mind, and every instinct in her screamed, *"No! Don't let him go! It's a trap!"*

The three of them huddled together.

In a low voice Nia said, "Enjo, can't you see it's a trap?"

"Nia, what could *Great House Amaterasu* want with me?"

"I don't know! But why else would they want you to go first? I don't think the most Harpy-hating family in Other Side would have a welcoming committee for you!" She hissed.

"It is pretty suspicious. But really, why would they want him to go first? I doubt the gates would be able to close fast enough for them to snatch up Enjo without us seeing. And it's not like we wouldn't- you know, *notice* he was missing," Ryoko said. A smile crept up her face. She hastily bit her bottom lip, but from how she was shaking it was clear she was holding in a laugh.

"What's so funny?" Enjo asked, insulted.

Ryoko burst out laughing. "The idea of it! *'Wow, the gates just closed! Oh, now they're open again! Huh, I wonder where Enjo went! Well, we didn't see him get snatched up by Great House Amaterasu like he was the last donut in the box, so I guess he wasn't!'*" Ryoko said, gasping for breath. Tears of laughter rolled down her face. Enjo gave a nervous, insincere chuckle.

"So are you kids going in or *what?*" The guard called down.

"Yes, we're going!" Enjo called back. He looked at Nia and Ryoko, and smiled.

"It'll be fine. We can't go in unless we follow the rules, and besides," He said, turning to the main gate and walking towards it, "I'm looking forward to seeing the home of my ancestors."

Ryoko gave Nia a confused look. Nia said hastily, "He has Fire Spirit ancestry. *Ancient* Fire Spirit ancestry. Before his family tree kind of dominated with Sound Spirits, then Harpies-"

Nia was interrupted by the sound of the gates clanging shut. She and Ryoko turned immediately to look, and to Nia's dismay, they were shut tight.

"No! Enjo!" She cried.

"What's going on?!" Ryoko demanded.

The guard on the wall ignored her. She was looking over the other side of the wall intently, and after a few seconds she barked at another guard, "Alright, open the gates!"

The gates swung open faster than Nia had expected. And in the silent Main Street of the Province of the Fire Spirits, Enjo was gone.

Chapter Nine
Burning the house down!

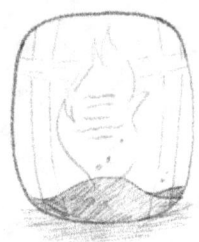

The first thing Nia did was panic.

She forced herself to breathe, then she became dimly aware of Ryoko yelling at the guard. *"What do you think you're doing?! Where is he?!"*

"Orders! And if you crazy kids say another word and don't go in right this second we're closing the gates!"

Ryoko growled. She and Nia hurried inside, and the huge gates swung shut behind them. As soon as they were inside Nia looked around frantically, but besides a bat-cat licking its wings near a clinic, there was no one there. The two of them sat down absently on a ledge of the main statue of the square: A Harpy on its knees, defeated, erected in honor of the Fire Spirit's victory in the First Phoenix War. The hopeless look in its eyes matched Nia's mood perfectly.

"What do you think happened?" Ryoko asked. Nia muttered, "We were right. It was a trap. And they got him."

"Well, we can't just sit here! We have to do something!" Ryoko said. She gave Nia a reassuring pat on the back. "We'll get your friend back, okay? I know we will."

Nia looked at her with her eyes glistening with tears, and wiped her eyes on the back of her sleeve. She nodded, and took out her travel book. After flipping through it she found a familiar map of the Province of the Fire Spirits, one she'd studied many times with fascination. "Here," She said, pointing to the home of Great House Amaterasu. "If Great House Amaterasu gave the orders directly and not through the city guard, it wouldn't be surprising if they wanted Enjo taken straight to them. Why? I don't know. But if so, we need to get there. Now."

"Then what are we waiting for? Let's go!"

About ten minutes later, they'd passed into a much more crowded area of the Province of the Fire Spirits and arrived at the home of Great House Amaterasu. The mansion rose up directly in the middle of one of the Province of the Fire Spirit's most prestigious districts, and the building was as grand and imposing as the Great House Amaterasu name. Nia and Ryoko looked up at it, then at the wall surrounding it. "So, what's your plan?" Ryoko asked. Nia frowned. "I don't feel good about sneaking into Great House Amaterasu in broad daylight, but it looks like that's what we're going to have to do." Nia glanced behind them. The square was bustling with Fire Spirits hanging lanterns and setting up stalls with food, and there was even a street performer using their Fire Magic to create miniature fireworks and juggle fireballs. The festivities sent a chill down Nia's spine as she remembered. *Only four days left until Eris' Day.*

She looked back at Great House Amaterasu, then Ryoko. "This won't be easy, but it'll be doable. Follow me."

After some examination, climbing onto a roof on the main building, or one of the other smaller buildings, was out of the question. They were all covered in tiny, almost invisible spikes. So, Nia led Ryoko to the back of the building and took out two metal claws that fit over her hands, something she'd packed especially for infiltrating the home of Great House Amaterasu if all else failed. She handed them to Ryoko before putting on a pair for herself. "I don't need these, they'd just slow me down. Wait, you know how to use these, right?" Ryoko asked.

"What, you think I've never broken in somewhere before?" Nia snapped. Then she fastened the straps for one of her metal claws and sighed. "Sorry, I guess the stress is getting to me."

"None taken."

The two of them scaled the wall, and when Nia was halfway up Ryoko had already disappeared through a window. "Ryoko! Wait!" Nia hissed. She scrambled up the rest of the wall and dropped noiselessly through the window and onto the floor. Ryoko was waiting for her in the elaborate hallway, and fortunately, there was no one else around.

The distinct feeling of threat, unease, and the caution they had to take hung over them like a shadow. Nia looked around. She couldn't hear anything and felt no presences, so she gestured for Ryoko to follow her. Nia kept her hands near her belt as she walked, or more specifically, her daggers.

"You're not going to go on a rampage and kill someone out of anger, are you?" Ryoko asked in a whisper.

"Probably not. Still, if someone finds us, we need to be ready to defend ourselves."

They continued, and as they passed a pair of large double doors Nia stopped, and remembered why the three of them had gone to the Province of the Fire Spirits in the first place. A plaque beside the door read "Phoenix Memorial."

The ashes of a Phoenix! She went towards the doors, and listened. She could hear anything, and she felt comfortable peeking inside. She pushed on the door, and it opened some.

It looked like a kind of artifact room, and the windowless walls were dimly lit with candles inside. Quickly she looked around, then she and Ryoko went inside and almost closed the door, leaving it open a crack. Nia looked around. In the middle of the room, illuminated by a soft spotlight in the middle of the ceiling, was a pile of dark powder in an intricate glass jar resting on a pillar, in a box of protective glass. Nia stared at it in disbelief, then she looked at the

plaque on the glass: "The last surviving ashes of a Phoenix."
Nia's heart jumped with joy. She'd found it! She went over
to it quickly, then paused. She wanted to steal it right there,
but she something made her stop. She forced herself to
think. She hadn't brought the right tools to steal it properly,
because she didn't have access to them in the Province of
the Earth Spirits. She had gloves, so she wouldn't leave any
fingerprints. And she had her daggers, which she could use
to cut the glass. But she didn't have the white powder
Namei had used before on missions to detect traps. And
even if she did, she didn't like the idea of that powder
getting mixed in with the ashes of the last Phoenix. There
had to be a trap. And if she triggered it now, it was likely all
of Great House Amaterasu and all their guards would be
there in moments. Or worse, the entire floor she was on
would go into lockdown. That had happened once on one
of Nia's missions with Enjo and Namei. A magic field had
surrounded every wall, window, and door in the building
they had been in, and Namei had warned them not to touch
the field. If they had, they would've been knocked
unconscious. Namei had to break through the field by force
and a secret technique, and Nia seriously doubted she was
strong enough for something like that. Ryoko, though- Nia
could see her smashing through a field easily. Then she,
Enjo, and Ryoko could escape. She had to rescue Enjo first
before an alarm could be raised, and retrieve the ashes
later. But then again- and this thought made Nia almost
shudder- there was a chance Enjo hadn't been captured by

110

Great House Amaterasu, and been captured by the Paradox instead. And if that was the case, Nia knew exactly where they would be now; whatever was left of him after the Paradox was through with him would be scattered throughout the Badlands, to be eaten by monsters and never seen again. The thought made her sick, and she pushed the possibility far away in her mind. But she kept it in mind, even though she wished desperately it wasn't true. She tugged away a corner of her right glove, and felt relieved to see that the Delta was still there.

"What is it, Nia?" Ryoko asked.

"We can't take it now. If we do there's a chance of blowing any chance we have of rescuing Enjo and getting out safely."

"Fine. You're the expert."

Nia stepped away from the ashes, wishfully. Then she turned, and sprinted out of the room and back into the hallway of Great House Amaterasu. She ran at full speed, light and swift on her feet and hardly making a sound. Ryoko followed close behind, but unfortunately, she was much louder. "Can't you run any quieter?" Nia hissed. "I'm *trying!* I haven't had any practice sneaking into places before!" Ryoko hissed back.

Nia turned abruptly when she reached a corner or staircase and the two of them went down, into the furthest reaches of Great House Amaterasu. She suspected to find some sort of basement or dungeon there, but when she reached the ground floor of the Amaterasu Mansion she was astonished to find one of the doors was wide open and a narrow beam of light was streaming out into the huge, unlit main room. Nia came to an abrupt stop and hid in the shadows, listening. She heard footsteps, then someone crossed over to the door from inside the room and hastily closed the door. She and Ryoko stood still, hardly daring to breathe, when they heard voices from the room.

"How long will it take?" One voice asked, in a low voice.

"Hours if I do it right." This voice was younger than the first, and female.

"What if Lord Enzo finds out?"

At first, Nia thought she had heard "Enjo." Then her mind corrected itself- Enzo. It was only one letter off from Enjo.

"Don't worry about the head of house. I'm sure once I'm done and it's on the table tomorrow morning, he'll forgive me. I mean, it's a delicacy! It's been eaten at secret ceremonies by the head of Amaterasu house for generations! It was worth forging those orders to the guards. All I had to do was do a little flick of my wrist for Lord Enzo's signature and they were tripping over themselves to obey."

"Alexandryn, they got rid of this tradition *ages* ago!"

"Yes, but they didn't want to. And do you know why?" There was a pause as she waited for her companion to respond, but he didn't. She went on, "Because the main ingredient got wiped from the face of Other Side two hundred years ago, that's why. Fire Spirits would eat this every day if they could, especially if I was the one to prepare it."

"Open your eyes! This is *cannibalism!*"

Nia's heart skipped a beat.

"It's not *cannibalism*. Cannibalism is when you're eating one of your own kind. This thing-" There was a yelp, and Nia recognized it immediately. *Enjo!*

"Is only *part* Fire Spirit. It sealed its fate when it tried to burn me to get away. Didn't you ever hear the phrase, 'don't fight fire with fire?'" She asked, addressing Enjo now. Another yelp. Nia's hands went to her knives, and a bead of sweat trickled down her neck. She had to be honest with herself, she was terrified. Whoever this psychotic chef lady was, she was the one who had kidnapped Enjo. And now she was getting ready to cook him into a dish for the head of Great House Amaterasu. She knew she couldn't waste a moment. She had to break into the room and rescue Enjo *now*. Nia wasn't afraid of the woman, or whoever her companion was. What she was scared of most was being too late, and breaking into the room just as the chef gave Enjo a killing blow. She set her jaw and gripped the hilts of her knives. If she wanted to save Enjo, she would have to act fast. Before Nia could move she felt Ryoko's grip on her shoulder, and she glanced back at her. Ryoko's eyes were shining with fierce determination.

"Don't worry about getting inside. I'll take care of the door," Ryoko whispered. Nia nodded.

"What will you do first?" The chef's companion asked, with a hint of nervousness in his voice.

"First I'll have to kill him so he won't move. Then I'll set him on the tray, cut off his wings- I'll sew them back on once he's cooked and ready to serve, like the traditional recipe."

Nia and Ryoko hurried to the front of the door. Ryoko gestured for Nia to stand back. There was the citrusy smell of oranges, then a spark of magic leaped off of Ryoko's right arm. Ryoko drew back her fist, and suddenly her eyes and the veins of her arms blazed with golden light; the color of Earth Magic. Nia braced herself.

"Next, I've prepared a mix of seasonings that should go nicely with it, so I'll-"

Suddenly the door to the kitchens exploded inwards at Ryoko's punch, and Ryoko and Nia burst into the room. Two shocked and astonished Fire Spirits shrieked. Enjo was lying on a kitchen island in the middle of the room, facing the door. He was gagged and bound in ropes, but his eyes lit up when he saw Nia. Nia was the first to react. She jumped forward and knocked a long knife from the chef's hand as she unsheathed one of her daggers, and in one move grabbed the other dagger from its other sheath and pointed both of her knives at the chef and her companion's necks, who Nia assumed was her assistant. They stood still, stunned. "Alright, both of you against that wall! And don't move!" Nia barked, trying to copy how Namei had acted in situations like this. The chef opened her mouth to argue, but her assistant hustled over to the wall obediently, then the chef followed. They stood against the wall facing her, silent.

Nia turned to Enjo, and cut through the ropes binding him. Enjo sat up and took off his gag, untying the cloth and spitting out some wet cloth onto the floor. He choked and coughed, trying to adjust. Nia wrapped Enjo in a hug. "I'm so glad we found you!" She said. *"They were going to eat me!"* Enjo said, shrilly. He seemed extremely rattled by the whole thing, and Nia couldn't blame him. She let go of Enjo and looked at the chef, whose face was set in a scowl. *"We weren't going to eat you, you were going to be a meal for the head of Great House Amaterasu!"* The chef said. Nia glared at her. "Do I really have to tell you to not speak, either?" She asked. The chef's assistant, an older Fire Spirit who looked kind but sorrowful, said, "I'm sorry. Once Alexandryn gets something in her head, she can't be persuaded otherwise."

The chef, Alexandryn, crossed her arms. "Hmph! Well, you shouldn't have rescued him. I would've made him into a-"

Suddenly the knife Nia had knocked from the chef came flying across the room, and lodged itself in the wall beside the chef's head. Alexandryn yelped and ducked moments after the knife had landed in the wall. *"I said, don't move!"* Nia barked. The chef was silent.

"And be happy I have a good aim," Nia added. "If I had a bad aim you'd be dead." Ryoko gave Nia an impressed nod. "Nice," She said.

Nia looked back to Enjo.

"Enjo, what happened?" She asked.

"I- I don't really know. As soon as I went through the gate they closed, then she grabbed me from behind and shoved something in my face!" He said, glancing at the chef angrily. The chef scoffed. "Don't worry, the knockout poison wouldn't have ruined your flavor."

Nia shot Alexandryn a glare, and she went quiet. After a moment Nia said, "Alright, I think I have a plan to escape. But I'll have to tell you on the way." She looked to the chef and her assistant. "You two are going to sound the alarm the second we step out of this room, right?" She asked. The chef sneered. "Of course I will! You're just some crazy kid that messed up my masterpiece and broke into Great House Amaterasu!" The chef's assistant looked at Alexandryn sharply. "No, you will *not* be sounding the alarm." *"What?"* The chef shrieked. *"Of course I will! I'm the chef, you're just my assistant! I'm the one that gives the orders!"* The chef's assistant gave her an appalled look. "Absolutely not! You nearly killed that child- we owe them both an escape!"

The chef snarled, and said nothing.

Nia gave the chef's assistant a grateful nod. "Thank you, sir. Enjo, Ryoko let's go."

Enjo approached the door, and as he passed her he whispered, *"Please don't kill them."* Nia gave him an insulted look. Ryoko followed Enjo out protectively, and shot one last threatening glare back at the chef and her assistant before leaving.

As Nia turned to go she felt Chef Alexandryn's hand grab her wrist, and she jerked her arm away. *"Don't give me an excuse to kill you."* Nia snarled. Alexandryn gave her a smug grin. "You have no idea what he truly is, do you?"

"I have a better idea than you do, Harpy-eater."

"You don't understand. Great House Amaterasu won't let that boy out of here alive, and when he's dead-"

"Why are you so obsessed with killing Enjo?" Nia snapped, grabbing the hilt of one of her daggers but not unsheathing it.

"Because when I cook the Head of House Enzo the best meal he's ever eaten, he'll give me back my place as head chef. And your friend *will* die, sweetheart. As long as he walks Other Side, he'll never be safe. *Because of what he is."*

Nia unsheathed her dagger. Her hand was beginning to shake with rage.

"You *monster.* How would *you* even know what he truly is?"

The chef rolled up her shirt sleeve, and Nia gasped at a raw burn that went up her entire arm. "He nearly burned me alive while I was trying to bring him here. I know he's a Hawkee, and a Hawkee can never exist in Other Side. Not since the First Phoenix War. They're abominations who were too powerful for their own good, and that's why all the Hawkees were massacred so long ago."

At the word "Hawkee" Nia's heart leaped to her throat in terror. A lifetime of keeping a precious and dangerous secret crumbled around her, and the terrors of "what if" returned tenfold. She forced away her fear and said as cooly as she could, "They *weren't* abominations. Hawkees were just Air Spirit and Fire Spirit hybrids."

Chef Alexandryn's golden eyes twinkled with a crazed look, and she leaned in close.

"You know what? I know what you are, too. *Hail Eris.*"

Nia looked into her eyes, opened her mouth to speak- and stabbed her dagger deep into Alexandryn's gut.

The twinkle in her golden eyes vanished and was replaced with complete shock. She stumbled backward and hacked up blood, coughing up the pearlescent liquid over the front of her chef's coat. Her assistant shrieked and ran over to prop her up, but otherwise wasn't very helpful. "Alexandryn? *Alexandryn!*" He cried. Her eyes closed as she slipped from consciousness, and the assistant eyes met Nia's. She was breathing heavily, and pearlescent blood was dripping from her blade and her chin from where Alexandryn had coughed on her. Nia wiped the blood on her chin away with the back of her hand, and gave the assistant a steely glare.

"I'm not about to put my friend in danger because I gave mercy to someone who didn't deserve it. You don't remember anything from this encounter, especially nothing about a Hawkee. Got it?" She snarled.

The assistant gave a petrified nod. Nia sheathed her dagger and crossed her arms, glaring down at the motionless body of Alexandryn. "She'll survive. The wound I gave her isn't fatal, and I coated my dagger with a memory-wipe and healing fusion potion. But take her to the infirmary before she bleeds to death." She snapped.

The assistant scrambled to pick up Alexandryn, and practically sprinted from the room.

Twenty minutes later, Nia met Enjo and Ryoko back at the artifact room.

Nia pushed open the doors to the room, and beckoned Enjo and Ryoko to follow her. She stepped into the room, scanning the walls and floors for any traps she might have missed earlier. She couldn't see any, and at first glance, the room looked exactly like how she'd left it. She gave a sigh of relief, then turned to Enjo. He was looking at the glass box with wide eyes. "Is that-?" He asked, pointing at the display.

"Yes, that's it. I know, I thought it was a pile of dirt at first, too." She said, now scanning the ceiling. "Now, I would've taken it earlier, but I didn't have the right tools. We still don't have the right tools, but if we steal it fast enough we might have a chance."

As Nia walked past him Enjo paused, and sniffed. "Is that blood?"

"It's nothing," She said, stiffly. "We need to focus on stealing the-"

Suddenly Ryoko grabbed Nia's wrist. "Nia, look!"

Nia looked at the display. The ashes of the Phoenix were gone. She barely had time to gasp before the floor was suddenly replaced with total darkness, and the three of them fell feet first into the void.

Nia woke up to the feeling of a bag being taken off her head, and she gasped for air.
She looked around wildly and stopped, dizzy. The room she was in spun, fuzzy and out of focus. Through the fog she thought she heard a door shut and lock. When the dizziness faded and her eyes adjusted, she looked around, slower this time. The room was dimly lit with orange candlelight, and she was sitting in a chair, tied haphazardly to it with rope. She was alone, and the room was as bare as a prison cell. Her heart sank when she realized that was probably *exactly* what she was in now. It wasn't like the prison cells she'd heard of, though- the walls were covered with sheets of metal, and it looked like some kind of storeroom. She was sitting in the middle of the room, and lining the walls were shelves upon shelves of labeled jars, boxes, and bins of ingredients. Tacked to a cork-board full of recipes, lists, and notes was a paper with the words "Tomorrow's Ceremonial Meal: Fire Flower." She stared at it for a moment, then turned her thoughts to the process of escape. Whoever had tied her up had clearly never taken anyone prisoner before, because the ropes she was tied in were mismatched and poorly tied. And they had made a fatal mistake- not confiscating her knives. She smirked, then jabbed her hands to the sheaths of her knives and pulled them out, and in one move cut herself free. The ropes fell off of her onto the

floor, and she stood. She sheathed her daggers, then rubbed her arms. Even if they hadn't tied her very well, they had tied her a little too tight for comfort. She was about to walk to the door when it was unlocked and thrown open, then Enjo burst in and leaned against the doorframe, panting for breath. "They're chasing me! We have to go!" He said. Nia didn't stop to ask who was chasing him. They bolted into the hallway and ran, and soon the sound of running footfalls came from the hallway behind them. Nia took the lead and Enjo followed her, but after a few minutes of navigating through the hallways and rooms underneath Great House Amaterasu, she noticed Enjo was falling behind. "Enjo, keep up the pace!" She called out. "I'm trying! I don't think this was designed for running in!" Enjo answered. Nia looked back. He was wearing an elaborate robe in traditional Fire Spirit style that went down to his ankles, and the fabric looked heavy and stiff yet elegant. It was one of the fanciest outfits Nia had ever been in the presence of, or even seen. "How did- how did you get *that?*" She asked. "They just handed it to me! They said I had to wear it before I saw the head of Amaterasu!" Enjo said. Nia and Enjo turned at a corner, and Nia nearly slipped on the wooden floor before quickly getting her footing and taking off after Enjo. "I thought it looked nice, so I put it on." He said, looking back. "I don't think they like that I took it with me, though!" Suddenly Nia and Enjo came to an abrupt stop, and nearly slid into a wall. They turned to face their pursuers, and three spirits turned the corner and hurried towards them. The three spirits stopped, and faced them. The spirit in the middle looked like they were nearing old age, and he was dressed in a robe similar to Enjo's, elegant but simpler. The spirits flanking him were guards, dressed in dark red armor. The guards looked confused, and they kept glancing at the elderly Fire Spirit. The elderly Fire Spirit's gaze never left Enjo as he snapped his fingers, and both guards stood at attention. "Cato, search the house for Head Chef Alexandryn and her assistant and silence them. No one can know about this. Azumae, stay here." One of the guards obediently turned away and left, and the other stayed. Nia wanted to make a break for it, but she didn't dare. She doubted she and Enjo could make it past them without hitting another dead end, especially with Enjo's robe slowing him down. Her eyes darted away from where the other guard had been to the elderly Fire Spirit, who stood up straight. "My name is Enzo, and I am the head of Great House Amaterasu. I don't want to harm either of you," He said, firmly.

"Then why did you capture-" She stopped. They *had* been the ones who had tried to steal the ashes of the phoenix. She bit her tongue, and waited for Enzo to continue.

"I apologize for how we've treated you, but you have to understand that the ashes of the last phoenix are a historical treasure, a reminder of one of the greatest tragedies in history. Great House Amaterasu has protected it for generations," Enzo went on. He talked like he'd prepared everything he said in advance. Nia's eyes narrowed. He was being suspiciously patient with them, and she didn't know why. But she didn't like it. Enzo paused, and his eyes lingered on Enjo's wings. "I haven't seen many wings like yours." He said. Enjo jumped and hastily tucked them behind his back, face as red as his wings.

"The color of your feathers is more vibrant than most. Most Harpies do all sorts of things to make their wings as vibrant and full as yours, don't they?"

Enjo didn't answer. Nia knew he'd always hated when someone mentioned his wings, especially strangers.

"The only wings I've seen like yours belonged to Harpy roy-" Enzo paused, his eyes growing wide with shock. Then he put his hands to his face in exasperation. *"He's ruined us all."* He murmured. Nia and Enjo exchanged glances, confused. Enzo snapped his fingers again, then pulled a black card out of one pocket. Nia and Enjo could only see the back of the card, but the guard could see the front.

Then Enzo looked to Enjo. "Enjo Kutana, and- your friend," he said, nodding to Nia, "I'm sorry." Then he turned and walked down the hallway. Nia and Enjo looked at the guard, and their eyes met hers. The guard grinned, and unsheathed her sword. As the guard pulled it out of its sheath an intense glow lit up the dim hallway. Magma dripped from black volcanic rock fashioned into a blade, and as the guard advanced the dripping lava melted holes into the floor. "Which one should I kill first? The bird, or the fish? I've got an idea. Sing for me, little bird, and I'll kill the fish first!" The guard laughed. Enjo's face flushed. Nia yanked open her water bottle. *"All right, you asked for it! Nobody calls me a fish and gets away with it!"* She snarled. But before Nia or the guard could attack the wall behind Nia and Enjo crumbled and Ryoko stepped out, blinking, into the dim hallway. "Nia! Enjo! I found you!" She cheered. Then she looked at the guard. And before the guard could raise her blade Ryoko ripped away a chunk of wall and threw it at the guard. It hit her square in the head, and she collapsed. Her blade landed harmlessly on the floor. Nia, Enjo, and Ryoko looked at her for a second.

"Is she-?" Enjo asked.

Nia and Ryoko exchanged glances.

"She's just- sleepy," Ryoko said. "Anyway, what are we waiting for? Let's get out of here!"

Nia and Enjo followed Ryoko through the wall, and Ryoko smashed the wall beside them. Rocks and dirt rained down to seal the exit, and they were plunged into darkness. Nia hesitated, but then Ryoko grabbed onto her hand and pulled, and the three of them raced down the tunnel. "Ryoko, how did you find us?" Nia asked.

"I woke up locked in a storage room and started smashing walls."

Enjo burst into jealous tears. *"Earth Magic!"*

Nia ignored him. "Did you run into any other guards?" She asked.

"I did, but after I threw one out the window the others stopped following me."

"Earth Magic!"

"Did they raise the alarm?" Nia asked.

"Probably. I accidentally knocked down a big statue in the trophy room, and that made a lot of noise."

"Earth Magic!!" Enjo wailed.

"Enjo, if you say 'Earth Magic' *one* more time I'm going to pluck out one of your feathers!" Nia snapped.

"Sorry! I just want super strength so badly now!"

Nia saw a light at the end of the tunnel. She bolted towards it and burst into the open, and fell down a steep hill covered in sharp rocks and boulders. She shrieked and put her arm over her face to protect it, and she rolled down the hill and came to a stop and the bottom. She watched Enjo stop at the top of the hill and carefully pick his way down, then Ryoko burst out of the tunnel and slid down. She helped Nia up. "We can't stop now, they'll be after us!" She said. The three of them took off, and once they'd made it to one of the outer districts, they hired a dragon taxi out of the Province of the Fire Spirits.

Nia let out a breath she didn't know she'd been holding as they saw the Province of the Fire Spirits recede in the distance behind them. In the saddle of their dragon taxi- a hulking Earth dragon named Mudd, who'd emphasized the double letter "d" in his name in case they decided to write him a review, he'd explained to them while the three of them had scrambled into his saddle- Nia, Enjo, and Ryoko sat in silence for a long while. It hadn't taken them long to fly away from the Province of the Fire Spirits, and as they flew above the clouds the night air chilled them and played with their hair. The full moon shone brightly, lighting up the saddle and everyone in it so well Nia could see her own shadow. She'd felt like celebrating as they were escaping, but now a crushing realization had hit her.

"I can't believe we didn't get the ashes of the Phoenix in time. We failed," Nia said. She looked down at her feet. There was a gloomy feeling over all of them.

Then Enjo smiled, and took the ashes of the Phoenix out of his robe. Nia looked up, startled. "What?! You got it? How?"

"When I escaped my room I passed the room with the ashes. They'd put it back on display, and I got it. The floor opened up again, but I was already flying out of the room."

"Wow. You would think that since the Harpies are their worst enemies, they'd think of something you couldn't easily escape by flying," Ryoko mused.

Chapter Ten
A princess in a tower!

One hour later, Nia, Enjo, and Ryoko were still in the saddle of their dragon taxi. Enjo was curled up in his wings asleep on one side of the saddle, and Nia and Ryoko were sitting against the opposite side of it. They were looking down at the Badlands underneath them, and every so often they saw the occasional movement of a monster dart out into the open, then run off. Nia and Ryoko watched the Badlands underneath them for a long time. Then Nia asked, "How did this place ever get like this?"

Ryoko frowned. "It used to be another province, until the Ancient Spirits decided to wipe it out."

"Wipe it out?"

"Yes."

"Why?"

"The spirits there were big problems. Pun intended," Ryoko added. "It was the Province of the Giant Spirits."

"What did the Giant Spirits do to deserve this?" Nia asked, appalled.

Ryoko started finger-combing her curly hair, and her long brown fingers nimbly drew her hair into a short braid. "Well, nothing really. But they were really dangerous to all the other spirits, since they insisted on being huge all the time. Eventually all the other spirits decided to drive them out, but they couldn't. Then the Ancient Spirits stepped in and destroyed their province in one blow."

Nia's eyes went wide, and she muttered, "With the Devastation."

There was a long silence as the weight of this sunk in.

"Why is it still like this?" Nia asked.

"I guess it was because this is the place the Devastation was first used, so it was more concentrated here. I heard that it looks even worse in the exact spot the Ancient Spirits released the first drop of Devastation."

Nia looked down at the land under them. She realized that if the Paradox got their hands on the Devastation this was what the world would become; a dry, lifeless place where only monsters lived.

She sighed, and slumped against the side of the satchel. She stared up at the stars and moon, thinking of nothing but feeling everything. Ryoko asked, "Hey, Nia? Why were you and Enjo working for the Paradox in the first place?"

Nia was quiet for a moment.

"My dad was the Water Spirit Leader. The Paradox has been chasing my family ever since the Assembly got overthrown, and two years ago, when Enjo and I were thirteen, they caught us. They took me and Enjo's parents and made us sign a magic contract that forced us to become members of the Paradox. We're forced to obey whatever the Superiors of the Paradox tell us, as long as we're in earshot. And as long as I'm bound by the magic contract, we'll be stuck for the rest of our lives."

"You're *Gakusei and Yuriko's* daughter?" Ryoko asked. Nia nodded, and Ryoko shook her head in amazement.

"Wow. But there's *nothing* you can do to get out of the Paradox?"

"No. Unless-"

"Unless what?"

Nia went quiet for a moment. Then she said, "Unless Enjo dies."

Ryoko's eyes went wide. *"What?!* That's horrible! How could the Paradox expect you to kill Enjo?!"

"They don't. They want me stuck in the Paradox for as long as I live," She said, bitterly, "So if my parents ever escape wherever the Paradox is keeping them, they can use me for blackmail."

Ryoko's expression darkened. "Ugh, that's terrible. I'm glad you escaped."

"So am I. Enjo tried to escape so many times I lost count. But it'd never actually worked until two days ago. It feels almost like destiny."

They were quiet for a while. Nia looked up at the stars dotting the sky, enjoying the breeze. "Sometimes, when I

129

think of my parents, I remember the taste of my mom's granola. Her granola wasn't like the dry, nutty stuff at the store- it was soft, gooey, and warm, and stuffed with chocolate chips and oatmeal like cookie dough, " She said.

Nia closed her eyes, and smiled. "I never knew what my mom and dad were going to say. They were both so goofy, and they always made me laugh."

Nia looked down at the Badlands below them, distantly. "I really miss them."

Ryoko gave her a sympathetic look. "Hey, don't worry! You'll see them again in no time. And when you do, you have to introduce me. Your mom's granola sounds great." She smiled, and Nia smiled back. "Thanks, Ryoko. I can't wait to see them again," She said.

They sat in silence, enjoying the cool breeze.

Then Ryoko said, "Do you know want to why I really wanted to come with you guys?"

Nia nodded.

Ryoko hesitated. Then she closed her eyes and said, "Ever since I was little I *always* wanted to be a Gatekeeper. In my eyes, they're professional adventurers. They do everything from stopping crime to guiding other adventurers on whatever journey they're on. Since my dad is the Premier of the Province of the Earth Spirits he's the head of the Gatekeepers, and when I turned fifteen I thought he'd let me try out. He did, but I nearly got killed in the second entrance exam. So he took me out of the exams and I haven't been allowed to try out again. I know he's just trying to keep me safe, but I really, *really* want to be a Gatekeeper."

Ryoko paused to fold her arms on the side of the satchel. She rested her chin on them gloomily.

"It's always been my dream, and honestly, I'm not good at much else," She said.

Nia blinked in surprise. "What?"

"I'm not the best at math or magic theory, and I'm terrible at sports. There's no other job in the world I'd want to have, and that's why I want to bring the Heart of the Mountain back so badly. I want to prove myself so I can be a Gatekeeper."

They sat in silence for a while.

Then Nia said, "I don't think you have anything to worry about."

Ryoko looked at her hopefully. "What makes you say that?"

"Well, first you saved me from the Sand Spirits. Then you helped me save Enjo and escape Great House Amaterasu with our lives. If that doesn't get you into the Gatekeepers, then… well, you'll always be a Gatekeeper in my book."

Ryoko smiled. "Thanks. I appreciate it."

Behind them Enjo stirred, and sat up.

"Enjo? You were awake all this time?" Nia asked.

"No. I woke up a few minutes ago. I need more moonlight." He answered.

He was holding the glass jar with the ashes inside to the light, and examining it carefully. Then he traced his fingers on the tiny words inscribed on the glass. Nia watched him silently read the message.

"So? What does it say?" Ryoko asked.

Enjo went quiet, and a moment later he read aloud, "'We preserve the ashes of the last Phoenix, an unnamed Hawkee found in the Province of the Fire Spirits. We preserve these ashes along with the memory of the Hawkees that were senselessly murdered by the Harpies, killers of their brethren's children. We preserve these ashes in this urn to preserve them, and all the horrors they stand for, so that they may never be forgotten.'"

The silence that followed was a solemn one. It'd been a provoking message, and in Nia's heart, she felt a stirring of empathy towards the Hawkees she'd read of in history books. She remembered how the entire Hawkee race, the hybrids of Fire Spirits and Harpies, had been eradicated one night- and no one knew who'd done it, or why. The Fire Spirits had blamed the Harpies. The Harpies had blamed the Fire Spirits. And when a band of Harpy thieves stole from the Fire Spirit Treasury, tensions snapped. The two Provinces declared war on each other, and in the years that followed they'd torn each other to pieces in the two bloodiest wars of Other Side's history.

Nia glanced at Enjo, and memories of all the times he'd ever breathed fire in a desperate attempt to escape or just warmed his hands to heat a can of jinkfruit soup flashed through her mind's eye.

To Nia's surprise, the silence was broken by Enjo. But he didn't speak. Instead, there was the familiar smell of peppermint in the air that announced the presence of his magic, and Enjo held out his hand face up. And to Nia's horror, a small flame jumped to life.

"Enjo!" Nia screamed. She looked quickly at Ryoko. Her eyes had gone wide with fascination, and in them, she could see the reflection of the quivering flame.

"Enjo, I stabbed that crazy dodo in the gut with memory wipe potion, and you turn around and spill everything to Ryoko?!" Nia yelled. *"She can't know you're a Hawkee! Nospirit can!"*

Enjo looked her in the eye and said,

"I'm tired of keeping secrets."

The certainty in his voice wasn't reassuring. Nia looked at Ryoko again. She was still breathless with amazement, but after a moment she murmured, *"Wow."* Then she blinked, and the spellbinding effect seemed to be broken.

"You're- a Hawkee? I mean, a Phoenix?" She asked.

Enjo nodded, and the fire on his palm disappeared.

"The first Hawkee to be born in over two hundred years," He said, quietly. He closed his eyes and added, "Everyone just assumes I'm a Harpy. So as long as I don't use my fire, no one knows. Only Nia and a few others know that I'm a Hawkee. It's a secret I've kept my entire life."

"What? Why?" Ryoko asked.

Nia grimaced, but Enjo looked unmoved.

"Because if spirits learn what I really am, they'll kill me. Spirits have never liked Hawkees because we're the most powerful hybrids, and they know it. Some spirits even said it would be a Hawkee who would end the world," He said.

"That's not a good enough reason to kill someone! It's not like you *chose* to be a Hawkee!" Ryoko said, angrily.

"You're right. I didn't choose," Enjo said. Then he added a bit sadly, "Misfortune chose me."

There was another silence. And this time it was broken not by the three of them, but by their dragon taxi.

"You do know I can hear everything you've been saying, right?" He asked.

"Take everything you just heard to your grave and we'll give you a good review on WingsList," Nia said, flatly.

"Deal!"

The three of them soon drifted off to sleep, although it'd been difficult for Nia. She trusted Ryoko to not betray Enjo's secret, but hearing Enjo say everything about Hawkees the two of them had agreed- in a silent, mutual agreement- to never speak of, had rattled her.

The next morning, Nia woke to a sudden jerking of the dragon's saddle. Nia, Enjo, and Ryoko were thrown to the front of the saddle and they scrambled to grab onto it. Their dragon taxi had stopped, and they quickly blinked the sleep out of their eyes and looked around. They had left the Badlands and their dragon taxi had landed in a field of grass. Surrounding them in the air on all sides were dragons. Their dragon taxi whispered under his breath, "Ugh, why now?" One of the dragons, mostly white with touches of blue, touched down in front of them. She was carrying a woman in a saddle on her back, and she obediently lowered her neck and allowed the woman to use the spikes along the back of her neck as steps as she walked down towards their dragon taxi.

Nia recognized her as a Moon Spirit immediately, because on her forehead there was the same white birthmark all Moon Spirits were born with- except instead of a full moon, hers was in the shape of a waxing crescent. She was astonishingly beautiful, with dark brown skin and curly black hair that went down her back. She was wearing an elegant white dress, and as she walked towards their taxi her dress remained sparkling clean as it touched the grass and dirt. But the most striking thing about her was hardly her beauty. It was how confidently she walked toward Mudd, and how he cowed under her piercing gaze.

The lady walked towards him, and sighed. She folded her arms, and the saddle they were in shook as he trembled. She stared at him for a few moments, then her blank expression shifted to a small frown.

Their dragon taxi suddenly threw himself onto the ground, and Nia, Enjo, Ryoko, and their packs were thrown from his back onto the ground behind the lady. She didn't move.

"Lady Yhui! I submit!"

He bowed low, wings tucked meekly at his sides. From where she'd been thrown Nia sat up and watched Mudd and the lady who he'd called "Yhui." Their dragon taxi was over two thousand pounds of scales, muscle, and claws- and

135

seeing him afraid gave Nia the impression that this woman was more deadly than he was. Nia watched her every move in awe, caught between wondering if she was a friend or foe.

Yhui watched the dragon for a few moments. Then she reached out a hand, and poked the dragon on the snout with her finger.

"Silence. If you cared about your life," she said, "then you wouldn't have betrayed the Dragon Queen."

The dragon looked at her in horror. Then he fell to the ground, dead.

Nia stared at their dragon taxi's corpse in shock. *How had she killed him?* Her eyes darted back to Yhui, who was massaging her wrist. She looked up at the dragons circling overhead, and at once the three dragons that had accompanied her swooped down and picked up their dragon taxi's corpse in their claws. They flew off, and Yhui turned to face Nia. "Now, for you three. Who are you?" She asked. Nia couldn't speak. She sat there surrounded by the contents of one of their packs, feeling like she'd just swallowed her tongue. Behind her, Ryoko scrambled to her feet. "I'm Ryoko Bayani, and this is Nia and Enjo," She said, looking at both of them respectively. "Who are *you? And how did you just kill our dragon taxi by poking him on the nose?!"*

Yhui smiled, and Nia relaxed some. She took that as a good sign.

"I'm Yhui, sister to the Queen of the Moon Spirits." She said, with perfect manners and an elegant way of speaking. "I was visiting my sister when her friend told me of an annoying little stone under her foot with the name of Mudd. I decided to go after this 'Mudd' myself so we could sit down to a nice dinner without my sister's friend going on about how many *problems* she had," Yhui paused to toss her hair over one shoulder. "As for how I killed him, it was standard Blood Magic."

Ryoko stared at Yhui in awe. Nia glanced over to Enjo, who looked just as bewildered as she was. "Captain Heyna," Yhui said, addressing the dragon she'd been riding on. "Do you have room for three more in your satchel?"

Twenty minutes later Nia, Enjo, Ryoko, and their packs were sitting in a saddle similar to the one their dragon taxi had worn, but this one was made of pristine white unicorn hide that was soft to the touch and showed every speck of dirt and ash the three kids had brought with them. Nia remembered the crusty brown leather of Mudd's saddle and the crude messages that'd been carved and scratched into it by former passengers. She didn't miss it.

Closer to the dragon's neck Yhui sat in a seat of her own. As they flew Yhui told them about Mudd and how he had betrayed the Queen, who happened to be her sister's childhood friend, by stealing records from the Dragon Palace and selling them. Mudd's customer had been caught, but Mudd had eluded capture by the Queen's royal guard

137

until Yhui killed him. "If I want something done right I do it myself," Yhui said, carelessly. Both Ryoko and Nia had been hanging onto her every word, and only Enjo was still tense in her presence.

"Your hair is really pretty!" Ryoko squeaked, overawed.

Yhui smiled, and flipped her perfectly curly hair over her shoulder. "So is yours, sweetie."

"What kind of hair potions do you use?" Ryoko asked.

"Oh, only Vivid. It's the only brand that works for my hair. But, that's enough about me. Let's talk about you three," She paused to give a wave of her hand, and three trays with steaming bowls of soup on them appeared. Against her better judgment Nia immediately dug in, and the hollow wail her stomach had been crying for the last half hour subsided. It was a creamy red soup with herbs, and the taste reminded Nia of the soup she and Enjo had with Namei the night before their escape.

Enjo, who'd been quiet ever since they'd climbed onto Captain Heyna, looked up from his soup and paused. "Oh!" He said, looking at Yhui, "I can't believe I didn't notice it sooner. Congratu-"

Yhui gave him a stiffening look, and he stopped. Nia and Ryoko exchanged glances, and Ryoko shrugged.

"So, how did you kids end up on Mudd?" Yhui asked, addressing Nia.

"We were just trying to leave the Province of the Fire Spirits, and he was the only dragon taxi available. He didn't- *seem* like a criminal," Nia said, lamely. "We were in a rush."

"What were you three doing in the Province of the Fire Spirits?" Yhui asked.

"We were trying to stop the Paradox. We stole the ashes of the phoenix before the Paradox could get them, and use them to destroy the world." Nia replied. The words were out of her mouth before she could think through them. Enjo added, "The Paradox is trying to bring the Devastation back into the world, and the ashes of the phoenix are an ingredient for it that they wanted. But as long as we have it, we think the Paradox won't be able to make it. We were on our way to the Province of the Sound Spirits to give them something- two things, actually."

"Give them what?" Yhui asked.

"This." Nia took the glass vial holding the ashes of the Phoenix and held it up. "The ashes of the last Phoenix. Oh, and the fabric of time," she said, gesturing to the dress folded tightly at the bottom of her satchel.

There was a moment of silence as the four of them looked at it. Then Nia said, "We were going to give the Geeta this to protect it from the Paradox. He's a childhood friend of my parents, and I've heard there's no province safer than the Province of the Sound Spirits if you want to protect something." In the back of Nia's mind her sense of caution was screaming at her. *No! Don't tell her that! What are you saying?!* But for some reason, she felt comfortable telling her. Yhui's eyes glittered as she looked at the glass urn. Nia

139

put it away. Yhui nodded and put one finger on her chin, thoughtfully. After a moment she said, "Tell you what. I'm in a good mood today, so I'll humor you kids. I admire you kids' commitment to doing this- trying to save the world and all on your own, innocent things- so I'll make a deal with you three. You do me a favor, and I'll tell you something about the Paradox."

The three kids looked at her in surprise.

"Wait, how do you have information on the Paradox?" Nia asked.

"Oh, just one of the perks of being the sister of the Moon Queen," Yhui said, carelessly.

"What's the favor?" Ryoko asked.

"I'll bring you kids to a tower. A lovely tower where a princess has been locked in for months, and your job will be to-"

"You want us to rescue a princess?" Enjo asked. Yhui's eyes narrowed dangerously.

"Don't interrupt me. As I was going to say, your job will be to defeat her."

Nia, Enjo, and Ryoko stared at her.

"You're… joking, right?" Enjo asked, clearly disappointed. Nia rolled her eyes.

Yhui watched him for a moment, then scoffed. "You kids tell me you're trying to save the world, and you have the nerve to ask me if I'm joking?"

She took a white fan out of her sleeve and opened it with a flourish, fanning herself lightly. "You would *think* riding on

140

a dragon would be less suffocating. The atmosphere here- it's overwhelming. The heat, especially. I don't understand how *anyone* can stand it." She murmured.

Nia wondered what it was like living in the Province of the Moon Spirits. With such a thin atmosphere, it was probably icy cold all the time.

After a moment Yhui opened one eye. "Well, what do you think? Will you accept?"

Nia weighed their options in her mind. They were only three days away from the date the Paradox was planning to destroy the world, and they couldn't waste a second. But Nia had no idea what Yhui knew- maybe she knew something about what the Paradox was planning next? Or even better- where her parents were being held? How to get in? That would be the best thing Yhui could tell her. She wanted to ask, but she had a feeling Yhui wouldn't just give up the information without them agreeing to defeat the princess, whoever she was.

It wouldn't take that long, would it?

But when Nia opened her mouth to speak, she sighed. "I'm sorry, but-"

"You and Enjo will agree to defeat the princess in battle, and I'll tell you about the Paradox," Yhui said, almost sleepily.

Nia and Enjo looked at her in surprise.

Then Enjo said, "I agree."

"I agree," Nia said. The words slipped out of her mouth in a moment, even though she hadn't wanted to say them. She hesitated, a weird feeling filling her mouth.

Yhui snapped her fan closed.

"Perfect. Captain Heyna, bring us to Princess Guinevere's tower."

The dragon they were on nodded, then they dived through the clouds toward the Other Side below. As they broke through the clouds below them parted, showing a beautiful tower in the distance.

Captain Heyna flew towards it, then touched down gently on the ground in front of it. Nia slid off her back and dropped onto the ground. She stared up at the tower, and started to analyze it. It was tall and thick, more like a squat castle than a tower, and the top looked large enough to house three dragons. The ground around it was a charming meadow, although some of it was scarred with black dirt and scorched plants. Nia looked at the strange scorch marks for a moment, confused. Then Enjo flew off the dragon's back and stood beside her. "Is that from a *dragon?*" He asked, voicing her thoughts. Behind them, Ryoko got off of Captain Heyna and Yhui answered, "Yes. That's from a dragon."

Enjo paled, and his wings started to tremble.

"Now now, if you three are really on such a tight schedule, I would *think* you'd be more eager to get this over with. Leave me in peace."

Then Yhui sat down again and made a gesture with one hand. A platter of fine chocolates appeared on a tray on one side of the satchel, and she began to eat.

Nia looked at Enjo and Ryoko, and tipped her head toward the tower. "Let's go, then." She said. The three of them walked towards the tower, and fortunately, the door to it was unlocked. They walked inside and up a tall, narrow staircase. "So, what do you think the princess is going to be like?" Ryoko asked.

Nia shrugged. "I don't know, but I'm not worried about defeating her." She said, stretching her fingers in preparation. Enjo was quiet as they went up the staircase, but as they approached the door he blurted out, "If the princess is stuck in there, why was the front door unlocked?"

He had a point, and Nia and Ryoko knew it. But neither of them had an answer for him.

After a moment Nia shrugged. "I guess we'll have to find out."

There was a short pause, then Enjo muttered, "I don't like Yhui."

Ryoko rolled her eyes. "What, are you *scared* Enjo?"

Enjo flushed as red as his wings. "What? No, it's her birthmark!" He stammered.

"What about her birthmark?" Ryoko snapped.

"It's a crescent moon."

"So?"

"The dark side of the moon on her birthmark means- that she's *evil,*" Enjo said.

There was a short pause. Nia exchanged disbelieving glances with Ryoko, and sighed.

"Enjo, that's a traveler's tale."

"But it's *true!* And besides, she keeps looking at me like she wants to kill me or something!"

Nia shook her head, and didn't respond. Instead, she grabbed the doorknob and pushed open the door, for this door was unlocked as well.

Nia stepped into the huge main room, and Ryoko and Enjo filed after her. The first thing Nia noticed about this room was how dark it was. She could barely even see the floor in front of her, and behind her Ryoko stepped on the back of her shoe and ran into her from behind. Nia stumbled. "Ow!" She yelped. "Sorry! Yikes, it's dark in here!" Ryoko said, hurriedly stepping away from her. There was the sound of a door closing and locking, and Enjo quickly turned and pulled on the doorknob. "The door's locked!" He cried, panicked.

"What? How?" Ryoko asked.

"I don't know! It's probably-"

Enjo was cut off by the sound of something scraping on the floor. All of them froze, and looked automatically to the source of the sound- the middle of the room. It was like the sound of many knives being dragged across the floor, cutting deep into the wooden floor and tearing it with every move. Then there was the sound of something huge

144

standing, towering above them. The three of them looked up, terrified, as a harsh blue glow began to fill the room. In front of them the long serpentine neck of a dragon glowed with power. Her eyes glittered fiercely, like diamonds in the darkness.

"I think," Enjo gulped, *"that* she's *the princess."*

Chapter Eleven
The Dragon Princess!

Nia's hands flew to her ears as a deafening roar filled the tower. It was so loud she couldn't hear it at first, she felt it. She felt it in the form of the floor beneath her groaning and the tower around her shaking. It filled her with terror, and all at once she felt the same primal fear her ancestors must've felt when the first dragons terrorized Other Side. She trembled and nearly lost her balance, but Enjo and Ryoko caught her before she fell. The roar ended abruptly, then the dragon fell onto four feet. She glared at them, her snout curled into an evil sneer, her glowing blue eyes and neck throwing shadows on the rest of her features. Nia couldn't think. She couldn't breathe. The dragon's snout was only feet away from them, and suddenly she puffed up her cheeks like she was about to vomit. *"Move, move!"* Enjo screamed, shoving Nia to the side and grabbing Ryoko by the wrist, diving to where he'd shoved Nia. Nia fell unceremoniously to the floor, smacking the palms of her hands against it as she tried to catch herself. Enjo and Ryoko tumbled to the floor beside her. Nia flinched from the pain in her palms and instinctively scrambled away, and behind her a wave of intense heat licked her ankles. *Bang!* The sound of something smashing into the door, then a brief sizzling sound, crashed into her ears. Nia's gaze went back instantly to where they'd been standing. The charred wood of the door had been blackened again from a blast, and smoke rose hissing from the door. Her eyes went back to the dragon, just in time to glimpse a shape race towards her middle. She rolled to her side, and the dragon princess' talon stabbed the floor where she'd been. Nia turned again and frantically got to her feet. The princess tugged her talon from out of the floor, and turned towards Nia again. She roared, then spun. Nia, Enjo, and Ryoko threw themselves to the floor as her tail whizzed over their heads. Nia felt her scales brush against her hair. Then she heard a clanking sound as multiple things were ripped from the walls and dropped with a clatter onto the floor, and Nia looked up from the floor to see that they were dozens of curtain rods-they'd been holding up curtains that had been drawn tight, blocking out all the light from outside. The curtains must've caught onto the dragon's tail as she spun, and now sunlight exploded into the tower and Nia blinked, dazzled, until her eyes adjusted. Even the dragon princess looked dazed from the sudden rush of light. She paused, blinking, and Nia saw

147

her for a moment in the full light. She was a beautiful, striking dragon with white scales and golden horns that sparkled in the light. Nia lay there, stunned. Then the dragon looked to Ryoko and Enjo, and the evil sneer returned. Nia quickly got to her feet. When her head was turned Nia ran towards the princess, and directed a stream of water towards her. She bolted towards her, but as she grew nearer the dragon princess turned and faced her. She snarled and lunged toward her, but Nia brought the stream of water out from behind her and the water smacked into the princess' mouth. She gagged from surprise and swallowed the water, then Nia grabbed the princess' snout, launched herself over her, and landed on her back. She grabbed a spike and held on, and the princess started thrashing like a bull to try and throw her off. Nia skillfully unsheathed one of her daggers and jabbed it deep in between one of the scales on the princess' back. The princess gave a shrill roar, and before she could smack Nia in the back with her tail Enjo tackled her off of the dragon's back and they rolled onto the floor.

He and Ryoko jumped up, and Enjo took a step forward.

Again the dragon princess took in a deep breath, and her cheeks filled with air. Enjo did the same. The dragon's jaw snapped open, and a bolt of lightning flew toward Enjo and Ryoko. "Enjo! Ryoko!" Nia screamed. Her hand raced to her water bottle, but she caught a glimpse of Enjo's wing and paused. He'd flown upwards with Ryoko in his grip to escape the attack, and now he threw Ryoko towards the princess' jaw. *"Ryoko! Now!"* He yelled. Ryoko slid down the stunned princess' upturned snout and grabbed onto the horns on her head. Then she turned and grabbed the dragon princess' upper and lower jaws in each hand, and wrenched them open. The princess roared in frustration.

"Open wide!" Ryoko yelled.

Enjo exhaled, and a torrent of fire exploded from his mouth. Ryoko let go just as the fireball hurtled into the princess' jaw.

The dragon princess sputtered, recoiling from the flames. Ryoko, still holding tight to the horns on the back of the princess' head, punched the dragon's snout with her free hand. There was a bone-shattering *crunch,* and the princess howled. She gasped and gagged, and smoke poured out of her mouth. She clawed the air frantically, and Nia, Enjo, and Ryoko covered their eyes with their arms, coughing, to block out the smoke. The princess flung her snout upwards, throwing Ryoko, and Enjo caught her in his arms moments before she hit the floor. He set her down, and Ryoko hurriedly pried a rock from the stone floor and threw it through the window. The glass shattered. When the smoke cleared they saw the princess clawing at her snout in pain. They watched as her eyes glazed over, and the princess tottered. She lost her balance and collapsed heavily onto the floor, shaking the entire tower and kicking up clouds of dust from the floor.

She lay in a heap, her wings spread limply over her like two sheets. The three of them waited for the last of the smoke to clear in a daze.

Enjo was the first to break the silence.

"Did I kill her?" He asked, tears pricking his eyes. Ryoko stared at him. "She tried to kill *us!*" She said. Nia blinked, and cautiously approached the motionless form of the dragon princess. She came right up to her side, and cautiously poked her with a stream of water. She didn't move.

Then Nia turned and said, "Her heart stopped."

Enjo's huge eyes became watery with tears.

"I killed her! I burned her insides to a crisp!" He squeaked. Ryoko sighed. Nia continued, "Well, we defeated her. I'm not crazy about killing her either, but she tried to kill us first, Enjo. We should go now."

They all looked back at the dragon princess.

"Nia?" Enjo asked.

"Yeah, what is it?"

"When dragons die, don't they start 'leaking?'"

"You mean, all the fluid in their necks that helps them breathe fire starts leaking out of their mouths? Yes, why?"

All three of them looked automatically at the princess. One of her eyes was open.

Nia's heart skipped a beat.

The dragon princess lunged, and in one move, scattered the three of them across the room. Nia hit the wall hard, and it knocked the wind out of her. She saw through bleary eyes

150

the dragon sneer at the three of them, then she advanced toward Nia. Her snout came closer, open slightly. She could see the dragon's white teeth flashing in her open jaw like daggers in her mouth. Her snout was only inches away. The dragon princess paused, then sniffed Nia. Nia saw wisps of her hair almost pulled into her nose, then fall. The dragon's sinister look returned, and she snarled. Then- to Nia's surprise- the princess' snout retreated as she stood to her full height. She looked down at Nia, and Nia stared up at her in shock.

"Aren't you going to kill me?" She muttered under her breath, reaching for a dagger on her belt. She hadn't been speaking to the princess- and she hadn't expected a response.

The dragon princess burst out laughing.

"Yes! *Yes!* Finally! Thank you! All of you!"

Nia blinked in surprise. *"What?"*

"Thank you! It's been so long since I've had the thrill of a *fight* like that!"

The dragon princess flapped her wings, and started pacing the floor as she went on delightedly. "I'm so pleased! That *thrill!* That *excitement!* You three were really fighting for your lives, weren't you? Yes, you didn't hold *anything* back! And you!" She said, looking at Ryoko, "That *punch!* I can still feel the sting!"

"Sorry, what's going on?" Ryoko asked.

The dragon princess blinked, confused. "What do you mean?"

151

"What I mean is, why do you seem *happy* that you just lost to us? You were ready to tear us to shreds a few minutes ago!" Ryoko said.

"For your information, *you* lost to *me*. Not the other way around. I've never lost a fight, and I don't plan to either."

Ryoko grumbled. The princess went on, "Anyway, you are the challengers my mother sent, aren't you?"

"What?" Enjo asked.

"The challengers! Mother said she'd have a treat for me while I was on holiday, but I had no idea it'd be a fight as great as this!"

Nia walked towards the princess, and crouched down beside her. "I'm sorry, what's your name again?" Nia asked.

The princess blinked in surprise. "You don't know my name?"

Nia shook her head. The princess gave her a regal look. "My name is Princess Guinevere of house Talon, heir to the throne of dragonkind. The three of you were fairly strong- for mortals- so you may call me Gwenna."

"I'm Nia Otohime Angdakila," she said. "And these are my friends, Enjo Kutana and Ryoko Bayani. We got sent here because a lady named Yhui-"

At the word Yhui, the dragon princess gave her an appalled look. "Yhui? You mean the sister of the Moon Queen sent you?"

"Yes, she did," Enjo said. "She made a deal with us, and if we defeated you-"

152

"*Defeated* me?" She roared. "Did she really expect you three to defeat me?"

Nia scowled, but said nothing.

"Well, tell lady Yhui that I'm done with my holiday. I should've picked the summer palace- I haven't been able to leave for *days*." The princess said.

"You haven't been able to leave? Why?" Nia asked. The scales on Gwenna's snout went red. "Mother hasn't sent a messenger, so I haven't been able to send her a message saying I want to leave. And I can't leave on my own. I forgot how," She said, stiffly.

"What? Can't you just break out?" Ryoko asked. "You don't think I *tried?*" Gwenna roared, gesturing to the scorch marks marking the walls with her snout. Nia and Ryoko exchanged glances.

"So, how are you going to get out?" Enjo asked.

Three minutes later Nia, Enjo, and Ryoko were sitting between the spikes on Gwenna's back, flying across the field beyond the tower and circling back toward Yhui and her dragon. Enjo still looked a little shaken by the sight of Ryoko punching through the wall of the tower, but the rest of them were in good spirits. "It's been a while since I felt the sun on my scales. It feels good!" Gwenna said, stretching out her wings.

They flew towards Yhui and her dragon and touched down, and the three of them slid off Gwenna's back. At their approach, Yhui looked up from her book (titled "How to

Pretend You're Reading." On its cover was a bright yellow sticker that read "275 million copies sold!") She closed it, and gave Nia, Enjo, and Ryoko a mild look of surprise. "Hm. So you really did defeat her," she mused. "And lived. That's quite a feat." She seemed almost disappointed that the three of them had succeeded.

"Well, we kept our side of the deal. What information do you have about the Paradox?" Ryoko asked.

"Not much, I'm afraid. However, there's a hideout that I know of that's quite near the Province of the Sound Spirits, located in the Malaka rainforest on the southernmost tip of lake Pines. There have been rumors of the Paradox putting that hideout under heavy guard, and if what you three say is true I can say with confidence that the ingredients of the Devastation are there. Princess Guinevere, I expect you'll be coming with us as well?" Yhui asked.

"Yes, I will. I plan to go through the Province of the Sound Spirits and back to the palace."

"Do you expect to find your mother there?"

"Yes, of course."

"Then I'm afraid you'll be disappointed. Your mother is having a conference with the Geeta and the Queen of the Harpies in the Province of the Sound Spirits." Yhui paused. "Your mother, my sister, and I were planning on meeting at her palace tomorrow morning. If you want to see your mother as quickly as possible I suggest you stay with us. I was on my way back to the palace after catching a criminal, and I plan to bring these three directly to the Geeta." She

154

said, looking to Nia, Enjo, and Ryoko as they climbed into her dragon's satchel. Gwenna squinted at them. "Really? Why?" She asked. Yhui came closer and explained in a low voice. A few minutes later Yhui climbed into her own satchel and Gwenna stood beside the dragon they were riding, ready to fly. Without a word they flew off, heading towards the Province of the Sound Spirits.

Chapter Twelve
The magic of music!

A few hours later they arrived in the Province of the Sound Spirits. Nia leaned over the saddle and looked out in amazement as a massive forest came into view on the horizon, and as they came closer the massive forest divided, creating a space wide enough for Gwenna and Yhui's dragon, and many other dragons, could fly through comfortably. They were flying through a forest, but it almost didn't feel like it. Here there were plenty of treehouses, if you could call them that. Buildings hugged enormous trunks and sat in the boughs of trees, and they were all modern-looking buildings that would fit in perfectly in Kazaki. Every so often there was a wide open space with more buildings or a garden or a farm. The sun was beginning to slowly set, and a beautiful orange light hit the trees and painted all the buildings built on them in calming shades. There were flowers, flourishing plants, and spirits walking everywhere. And everywhere, there was music. They passed one grove of trees to hear one song after another, and there were many Sound Spirits out carrying musical instruments. Some of them were using their instruments to do magic, and as they flew by Nia caught a glimpse of one Sound Spirit playing a synthesizer to fix the wiring of a lamppost. Spirits were singing and making music everywhere, and even though the sun was setting, they were still going strong. Nia had never heard anyone sing in public in Kazaki unless there was a big event, but here singing in public seemed like a normal and accepted thing. She smiled and absently leaned against the saddle, enjoying the ride.

The two dragons flew through the trees, and at Yhui's command, landed on a huge tiled landing deck. The building built into the tree was one of the most elaborate Nia had seen. She, Enjo, and Ryoko slid off of Yhui's dragon's back, and Yhui stepped down after them. Gwenna followed the four of them to the huge double doors of the building, which were big enough for even Gwenna to go through comfortably. Sitting in a chair beside the door, next to a small table with a whirring fan, was a tired-looking guard holding a book (Titled "How to Pretend You're Reading." On it was a bright yellow sticker that read "300 million copies sold!" Next to it was a red sticker that read, "Soon to be a documentary!")

"Name, please?" The guard yawned.

"Yhui Ellis-Tranquility of the Moon Spirits."

The guard blinked. "You're not on the list," He said, after glancing over his chalkboard.

"Of course I'm not. I didn't schedule my meeting with the Geeta beforehand," Yhui said, calmly.

"Then why are you trying to come in?"

Yhui smiled. "I'm here to see the Geeta. The princess wishes to see her mother, and I'm escorting three children with important information to the Geeta."

"These children?"

The cheerfulness of Yhui's smile flickered.

"What other children would I be speaking of? Those children?" She asked, gesturing to a group of children walking below the trees in the distance. The irritation in her voice was clear. "Now, are you going to keep the princess of the dragons waiting any longer?" Yhui asked. Gwenna scowled, giving the guard a hard stare.

"Sorry, miss, but I can't let any unauthorized spirits inside. I'd lose my job." The guard said, closing his clipboard decidedly. Gwenna snarled, and took a step forward.

"Now now, Princess Guinevere. Don't blame the guard." Yhui fanned herself lightly.

"Look, just let us in!" Nia snapped. "We can't wait any longer, the entire world is at stake!"

"The entire world? I doubt that. But look, just go ahead. But if you're here to commit a crime or something, a guard named Rey let you in." The guard said.

Yhui glanced at the guard's name tag, which read "Shelton" in bright red letters. The guard shrugged. "What? I don't like the guy."

Yhui didn't respond, and without a word she herded the four kids inside.

She led them across the floor of a polished, empty lobby to another pair of double doors, and opened them without hesitation. It opened into a huge conference room, and seated at a round table was the Queen of the Dragons, the Queen of the Harpies, and the Geeta Sebanu. They all looked automatically as the door opened, and the Dragon Queen gasped when she saw her daughter. "Guinevere?"

"Mum!"

Gwenna rushed over and put one leg around her mother in a hug, and the Queen smiled. She looked almost exactly like Gwenna, except she was much larger and lacked the blueish "freckle" scales that dusted Gwenna's snout. "Sweetheart, how has your holiday been? Good?" She asked.

Gwenna nodded. The queen smiled and went on, "I can't even *begin* to describe how busy I've been. It's drained the energy from me like mad. Did you fly all the way here?" She asked. Gwenna nodded, and the Queen gave her a concerned look. "Run along now then, and get something for yourself from the banquet room." Gwenna nodded again, smiled, and left. Yhui cleared her throat. All of the leaders looked at her, and she introduced Nia, Enjo, and

Ryoko. "They've just come from Princess Guinevere's tower to deliver important information to the Geeta and his allies," she finished. Nia and Ryoko curtsied, and after an encouraging nudge in the side from Yhui, Enjo bowed.

The Dragon Queen gave a nod of acknowledgment, Geeta Sebanu's eyes gleamed with pleased recognition when he saw Nia and Enjo, but the Queen of the Harpies- a Harpy woman with fair skin, long white hair, brilliant wings, and a matching peacock-feather hairpin and dress- haughtily looked them up and down without a word.

Yhui led Nia and Enjo to Sebanu. He looked just like how Nia had remembered him. His hair was black, and one side of his face was marked by black music-note birthmarks typical for Sound Spirits. He was wearing an official-looking cloak, and when he stood up Nia noticed the gitara strapped to his back.

He looked pleasantly surprised, but there was concern in his voice.

"Nia? Enjo? What are you two doing here?" He asked.

"We came here to give you two things, and we need you to keep them safe. As long as they stay in our hands it's not safe. But more importantly, the *world* isn't safe." Nia said.

She took the ashes of the Phoenix out of her satchel. Sebanu looked at the small jar and gasped, and Yhui's eyes glittered as she looked at the small pile of ashes.

"The ashes of the Phoenix- how?"

"We stole them from Great House Amaterasu," Enjo said.

"But why?"

"The Paradox is planning to recreate the Devastation, and if they get their hands on the ashes of the last Phoenix or the fabric of time then they'll have two irreplaceable ingredients that they need," Nia said. She took out the folded fabric of time as well and offered it to Geeta Sebanu.

Sebanu took the two items and seemed at a loss for words. "I see. It makes sense with the seemingly random movements the Paradox has been making."

He looked to Yhui. "If you'd like to join Princess Guinevere in the banquet hall one of the chefs would be happy to make you a plate of something," He said.

"Thank you, but I must decline," Yhui answered.

"Well then, I'd like to discuss things further with the Queen of the Dragons and the Queen of the Harpies. If what you say is true my two strongest allies deserve to know as well." Sebanu said. Then he said firmly, "You're excused."

Yhui gave him a piercing glare, then turned and left the room.

"Queen of the Dragons, Queen of the Harpies, Nia Angdakila and Enjo Kutana have brought us vital information, and if it's true, then it affects not just our three provinces, but all of Other Side," Sebanu said. He sat down in his chair, and beckoned Nia, Enjo, and Ryoko to sit down as well. They took their places in three of the many vacant chairs circling the table.

"What do you feel is so important that you say it affects all of Other Side?" The Queen of the Harpies asked.

161

"They've taken precious information from the Paradox, whose movements the Province of the Sound Spirits has been tracking. This information says that the Paradox has been gathering the ingredients for the Devastation and is planning to use it to destroy all life on Other Side."

The Queen of the Harpies paled. The Queen of the Dragons snarled.

"Impossible!" She roared.

"It's from the Great Deceiver's private files. And I have no reason to doubt the word of Gakusei and Yuriko's daughter, and her close friend."

"Then we must take action at once." The Dragon Queen said.

"But what should we do? The Paradox is too widespread for any certain course of action," said the Queen of the Harpies.

"I've already decided. I only felt that my two strongest allies deserved to know my chosen course of action, and why I have chosen it."

"Then please explain, Sebanu. We're listening."

"These children have entrusted me, and the Province of the Sound Spirits, to protect the ashes of the last Phoenix and the fabric of time. With the limited information that we have, I believe that protecting the ashes would be the most efficient route until we have another strategy."

"But what about the Fire Spirits?" the Queen of the Harpies snapped. She continued, "Allowing the thieves of the ashes of the last Phoenix into your Province without even a slap on the wrist, *withholding* the ashes from the Fire Spirits-they'll think it's despicable! Before you know it they'll suspect our three provinces of conspiracy, and they'll be waging war against your provinces as well as mine!"

"They can *try,*" the Dragon Queen scoffed.

"I understand your concerns, Hera, and if the Fire Spirits suspect the Province of the Sound Spirits for withholding the ashes I'll take full responsibility." Geeta Sebanu said. "But in the meantime, I plan to keep the ashes of the Phoenix and the fabric of time under close guard. And with them under my protection, I suggest we exert more of our resources towards rooting out the Paradox and stopping them permanently before they cause any more damage."

Enjo stood. Automatically all eyes were on him, and he froze for a moment. He stood straight and said in a clear, decisive voice said, "I have something to say."

Nia raised an eyebrow. She'd never seen him take charge like this before.

"Oh?" The Queen of the Dragons asked.

Enjo nodded. "Yhui, the sister of the Queen of the Moon Spirits, told that she knew about a Paradox hideout that would be likely to be holding one or more of the ingredients for the Devastation, like the Heart of the Mountain," Enjo cleared his throat and added, "I don't trust Yhui."

"Why is that?" The Dragon Queen asked, visibly offended.

"Because I think Ms. Yhui is a Superior of the Paradox."

Chapter Thirteen
Betrayal!

Enjo! No, not this again! Nia screamed in her thoughts.

"A Superior of the Paradox? What makes you say that?" The Dragon Queen asked.

"Because two years ago I was forced to sign a magical contract. It forced me to obey anyspirit in the Paradox, no matter what the request. And when we met Ms. Yhui, she ordered us both to do something and we obeyed, even though it was clear neither of us wanted to."

Nia blinked in surprise. Now that she thought about it, she *had* been about to turn down Yhui's offer. Then Yhui had worded her request as an order, and she and Enjo had agreed.

"Yhui is a very commanding spirit. Are you certain that you obeyed because of the contract?" The Dragon Queen asked.

"I'm certain. I've felt the physical effects of the magical contract, and I felt the same when she gave me that order."

The Queen of the Dragons snarled. The Queen of the Harpies listened with interest. Enjo went on, "And anyway, she fits everything that I would expect in a Superior of the Paradox."

"You suspect that she was attempting to lay a trap by giving you that information?"

"Yes. I don't think that her information is false, but that she's giving it freely in ill intent," Enjo said. Sebanu was sitting very still with his hands folded and his head forward, eyes closed in thought. Nia expected him to speak, but he stayed silent.

"My plan," Enjo said, slowly, "was for me and Nia to cautiously investigate this hideout. Nia and I know the layouts of hideouts well, and we were trained by the Superiors themselves."

"Absolutely not."

Nia and Enjo looked at Sebanu in surprise. "Neither of you are going. If Yhui really is a Superior for the Paradox, the two of you going to the hideout would be exactly what she wants."

"Why would she want us?" Nia asked. There was a short silence, and the Queen of the Dragons and Sebanu exchanged glances. The Queen shook her head slightly, and Sebanu sighed. He looked back to Nia and Enjo. "The punishments the Great Deceiver inflicts on the Listed are unspeakable." He said. He opened a drawer on his side of the table, and after looking through some papers slid a piece of paper toward Nia and Enjo. It was handwritten in tiny print, and at the top were the words "The Listed." Nia hurriedly scanned the list, confused, and stopped in horror at the last name: *Enjo Kutana*. "I can't let either of you back into the presence of Yhui or be allowed to go to that hideout," Sebanu said. "I'll go myself."

"Why is my name the only one on this list?" Enjo asked.

"We don't know. Nia has, of course, a bounty on her head. But the Great Deceiver only put Enjo on the List."

Nia looked down at the paper, and a mental battle whirled through her thoughts. Now she understood why the Sand Spirits had taken her, and why Chef Alexandryn had told them "as long as he walked Other Side, he'd never be safe." The Sand Spirits had wanted the bounty, and Enjo had been Listed.

But why had Enjo been Listed? Why not both of them?

Her resolve to infiltrate the hideout crumbled. Seeing Enjo's name on the List changed everything.

"Fine. I accept your choice." She handed him the paper again. Enjo gave her a look of shock. "We're *not* going to infiltrate the hideout?" He asked.

"No. We've done all we can, and now we can let the adults do the rest."

"You're wise beyond your years, Nia," Sebanu said. "I'll go to the hideout as soon as . Anything to add?" He looked at the Queen of the Harpies and the Queen of the Dragons. Neither of them said anything. "Conference dismissed," Sebanu said. The Queen of the Dragons stood up and left, then the Queen of the Harpies disappeared. Sebanu stood up and left the room and Nia and Enjo followed him out. "Nia, Enjo, Ryoko, I'll arrange for the three of you to have rooms in the guest house. Gwenna will be staying with her mother in the royal suite," He said. "I want you three to rest. Get your strength back, and while you do, you're safe in the Province of the Sound Spirits."

Nia, Enjo, and Ryoko followed Sebanu out of a door and along a small bridge. He led them to a small guest house and arranged for them to have comfortable rooms. Nia was led to her room by a maid, and as soon as the door closed behind her she pulled off her grimy traveling tunic (which was still covered in a layer of dust that seemed determined to not come off), threw herself onto the bed, and closed her eyes.

Nia woke up in the middle of the night, and the only thing she could remember from her dreams was the sensation of falling. To her, it felt strange knowing that the ashes of the Phoenix and the fabric of time were no longer secure in her backpack. It felt like she, Enjo, and Ryoko were at the end of their journey, like heroes at the end of a traveler's tale. But she didn't really believe that. She didn't feel like a hero; she felt like she'd been on a long, exhausting hit-and-run mission against the Paradox, running for her life and trying desperately to do anything she could to stop them. And yet, inside her she felt right. It felt good knowing that she'd done what she'd had to do. And with that thought, she rolled over, pulled the blankets closer, and closed her eyes.

But they opened a moment later at the feeling of someone shaking her by the shoulders. She shrieked and nearly struck out, but she hesitated as the spirit shaking her spoke. Nia recognized her immediately.

"Lady Yhui?" She gasped. "What are you-"

"Nia, listen to me!" Yhui hissed. "You're not safe here!" Nia wriggled out of her grasp and scrambled away from her. She felt ready to attack her, but the look in Yhui's eyes made her stop. The look in her eyes looked genuinely panicked and horrified. She stopped. Yhui continued, "Nia, please listen to me. You need to run! You should get dressed and leave, now!"

Nia tensed, anticipating the effects of the magic contract. But she felt nothing. To Nia's surprise, she realized Yhui seemed to be purposefully wording her requests so Nia wouldn't be forced to carry them out.

"Are you a Superior of the Paradox?" Nia asked. Yhui hesitated. "I am," She said, slowly. "But please, don't think that I am by choice. My abilities caught the Paradox's attention years ago, and I was forced to sign the contract. I've been serving them against my will in secret for years. The Paradox is launching a full-scale attack *right now*. Every available operative and Superior has been gathered to strike against the Province of the Sound Spirits"

She closed her eyes, looking pained.

"Nia, I've never had a chance to get away. But you did. You escaped, and please, don't let Namei's sacrifice be in vain."

"Namei's sacrifice?" Nia asked.

"The Superiors ordered her to kill you if you tried to leave. If she hadn't done what she did then you'd be dead by now."

A terrible feeling of dread grew in Nia's gut.

"She killed herself so she wouldn't be able to hunt down you and your friend," Yhui said.

Nia froze. She stared at Yhui with a horrified look. Then her grip on the sheets tightened. "Why are you telling me this?"

"Because this is my way of striking back at the Paradox. The Paradox wants you dead. Sebanu wants you dead. You're safe with no one, not even me."

Yhui's eyes darted to the window. "I have to leave. I won't force you to go, but if you want you and your friends to live, you'll listen to me."

"Wait, why would *Geeta Sebanu* want me dead?"

"I don't know. But it's the truth. *You have to trust me.*" Yhui said. Then she grabbed Nia's hands, and held them. Tears pricked her eyes Yhui's.

Something inside Nia cracked. Suddenly she wanted to trust Yhui with all her heart.

Or- *almost* all of her heart. She dismissed a tiny voice of doubt, and smiled at Yhui.

"I trust you," Nia said. Then she added, "You remind me a lot of my-" She stopped, startled. The realization hit her in a split second. Yhui was a Superior of the Paradox. And that meant that she might know something about her parents. Nia opened her mouth to ask, but she blinked. And at that moment, Yhui was gone.

Nia sat there for a few moments, digesting everything Yhui had told her. Then she got out of bed, stepping deliberately and silently across the floor, and pulled on the outfit that had been laid out for her. It was a traditional Water Spirit outfit for girls her age, and as she pulled the tunic over her undershirt its fabric smelled of perfume. The tunic and pants were a little more formal than she would've liked if she'd had to pick out an outfit to escape the Province of the Sound Spirits in, but they would do. She put her pack on her back and slipped her feet into the specially-made shoes they'd laid out for her, tied her hair back and pulled on the mask she kept in her pack, and went out the door.

It didn't take long to find Enjo's room. When she came to his door and listened she heard the faint, harmonious sound of his snoring, like birdsongs. She rapped on his door with her knuckles, and a few moments later she heard the shifting of blankets and Enjo shuffling drowsily across the floor to open the door. He opened it a crack and looked out.

"Enjo, you really shouldn't open the door for everyone like that." She hissed, annoyed.

"I could tell it was you!" Enjo said, defensively, "I saw your feet under the door."

"How could you tell they were my feet?"

"No one else here as flipper feet."

Nia wanted to point out that he hadn't had time to check everyone's feet, but she knew they were running out of time.

"You need to listen to me. We're in mortal danger right now."

"When are we not?" Enjo asked, sleepily. He rubbed his eyes with the sleeve of his pajamas.

"Enjo, I'm serious. The Province of the Sound Spirits is about to be attacked by the Paradox, and we need to leave, now."

"I'm tired. Can we joke around in the morning?" He asked, yawning.

"I'm not joking!"

"Ha, ha. So where are we going now? The Province of Conclusions? I heard you get there by jumping."

Nia wanted to strangle him. The entire Province of the Sound Spirits was about to be obliterated if they didn't do something, and he was joking. Enjo yawned again, and then his eyes lit up.

"Do you think they'll give us cinnamon rolls with our breakfast in the morning?"

"Enjo," she said, pointing at him, then the room behind him. *"Get dressed. Get your pack. And get out. NOW."*

Enjo looked at her, confused. Then he shrugged, and closed the door. "And bring a piece of paper and a pen!" She added.

Nia paced the hallway, pausing occasionally to listen for anything that sounded suspicious. Three excruciatingly long minutes later, Enjo was out of his pajamas and wearing a traditional Harpy shawl with his pack on his back.

"Alright, so where are we going, really?" He asked, stretching. "We're going to Geeta Sebanu," Nia said, turning and walking down the hallway decidedly. Enjo hurried after her, matching her silent footsteps seamlessly. Even with the talons on his feet, he could walk silently when he wanted to. "Why?" He asked.

"Because the Province of the Sound Spirits is about to be attacked! If there's anyone who needs to know that, it's him! We're not going to tell him that directly, though."

Nia reached the end of the hallway and a window. She felt along its edges, then pushed it open. She gauged the drop outside of it to be five feet, and she motioned with her head for Enjo to follow her. She squeezed through the small opening the open window made and jumped, landing noiselessly on her feet and one hand. She moved, and a moment later Enjo landed where she had been. She looked around. Now they were in a walled garden, and she quickly sprinted across the garden and leaped over the low wall. Enjo followed, and soon he caught up with her.

"Alright Nia, what's going on?" There was a hint of franticness in his voice.

"We're going to Geeta Sebanu to warn him."

"Of what?"

"The Paradox attacking!" She said, exasperated. "Weren't you listening!?"

"Nia, we're in the toughest Province in Other Side! You're being paranoid!"

"No, *you're* being too comfortable. Yhui broke into my room and told me. She risked her life!"

"She broke into your room?"

"Yes, and she told me the Paradox was going to attack any minute now! So we need to warn Geeta Sebanu as soon as possible so he can organize the Sound Spirits!"

"What about Ryoko? And Gwenna?"

Nia stopped, and Enjo came to an abrupt stop beside her. *"Ryoko! Gwenna!"* She said, horrified. *"We need to warn them!"*

"But where are they staying?"

Nia was about to answer she didn't know when her eye was caught by a sudden flash of light through the trees. Nia raised her head to look automatically, and she watched a sparkling light- like a lavender shooting star, only slower- rise into the sky and vanish. A feeling of raw horror filled her gut, and she looked to Enjo. He met her gaze with a horrified look, then mouthed, *The Paradox?* Nia glanced back at the sky. Three more sparkling lights followed the first, and a shriek filled the night. Then another light leaped into the sky, closer than the others. Nia looked back at him and grabbed him by the shoulders. *"Enjo, go warn Geeta Sebanu!"*

"No, Nia!" He pushed her hands away. "I'm staying with you!"

"Enjo, I'm not asking you. You have the paper and pen. You can-"

"What paper and pen?"

173

"You didn't hear me?"

"I wasn't listening! I was tired!"

Another scream. Closer.

"Don't argue with me, Enjo! If you don't have the paper and pen you go warn Ryoko and Gwenna! I'll go and tell Sebanu!"

"But I promised to protect you!"

"Go protect Ryoko and Gwenna! You know where to go afterward!"

In one move she stepped past Enjo and shoved him behind her with one arm, then took off into the night. She heard Enjo call out after her, *"Nia!"*

Nia jumped over the ledge of one bridge and plummeted ten feet, landing in a roll on the bridge below the first. As soon as she was on her feet again she was running, tracing the route she had to take in her mind. *Right. Straight. Left. Up.* She scrambled up a staircase. *Right again.* As she ran through a posh avenue that cut right through a huge garden she felt grateful she'd spent so much time studying the maps in her Travel Guide. The pristine stone path led up to a grand house. *Up again.* She hurried up the steps of the house, and pounded on the doors. *"Geeta Sebanu! Geeta Sebanu!"* She kept pounding on the doors, and she stopped abruptly only when the doors opened. A Sound Spirit attendant stood at the door, and peered at her.

"Yes?" He asked. "What is it?"

174

"I need to tell the Geeta something, *now!* The Paradox is attacking! I was told that they would attack any moment, and I counted five deathlights in the sky on my way here!"

"Who told you that they would attack?"

"Yhui did. She's a Superior of the Paradox, and I don't doubt her word."

He closed his eyes for a moment, then said, "You should go back to the guest house. We have this under control."

Does he really expect me to just "go back to the guest house?" Then the realization hit her. If most of the Paradox was attacking here, there wouldn't be as many guards at the hideout with the ingredients for the Devastation. She hated to leave Enjo, Ryoko, and Gwenna who she'd started to consider a friend, without a word, but she felt like it was the right thing to do. When would she ever have an opportunity like this again? She knew that as long as Enjo made sure Ryoko and Gwenna were safe, then she'd see them again before long.

She nodded, and silently turned and walked away. Once she was out of sight she ran off, out of the Province of the Sound Spirits, over a huge fence, and into the rainforest.

Once she was in the rainforest she slowed her pace, but still hurried. She knew she still had limited supplies and she didn't want to exhaust herself. She didn't know how much time she had, but she expected that she'd have two hours of traveling at the pace she was going before she arrived at the hideout, if what Yhui said was true and that the hideout

175

was really on the southernmost tip of Pines lake. Even though the Sound Spirits' forces were depleted because some were providing backup to the Harpies in the war and the Paradox was attacking with full force, she doubted the fight would last long. The Sound Spirits had a reputation for being the strongest province for a reason. But that made her wonder. From what she knew about the Paradox, unless they had a hidden card, they wouldn't throw away their best fighters in an impromptu attack against the Province of the Sound Spirits for no reason. They had to have a reason for attacking. She knew that they'd tried to attack the Province of the Sound Spirits before, but she didn't know why they'd wanted to attack then either. She wanted to think more about this, but decided not to. She needed her mind to be clear, especially if she was going into Paradox territory for the first time as an enemy. The forest was dissolving rapidly into rainforest all around her, and the ground underneath her feet was changing from the dark dirt and scattered pieces of wood of the forest she'd left behind to vivid green underbrush and exotic plants. The air smelled heavy of fruit and above her huge trees, the same height as the ones in the Province of the Sound Spirits but drastically different in shape, towered above her. Even very early in the morning when the forest was still dark and she couldn't see any light, natural or artificial, birds were chattering and singing through the night. The sound comforted her some, and she was reminded of Enjo. She knew he'd make sure Ryoko and Gwenna were safe. And now, it was her responsibility to keep herself safe.

She paused, scanning the area for any traps. She'd read somewhere, probably in her Travel Guide, that the Sound Spirits lined the area around the fence dividing the rainforest and the Province of the Sound Spirits with traps to keep the animals at bay, but she didn't know much about the traps. She knew plenty about the animals, though. When she was younger and her parents had homeschooled her, she remembered filling out dozens of tests about the animals of the rainforest. She'd always found it fascinating, because it was almost like another Province of the Water Spirits. It rained almost constantly, and the absence of rain now made her feel certain that it would rain at any moment. The ground under her feet was wet with dew and very earthy, and dew slicked the surface of every plant she saw and left puddles scattered across the ground. She continued hurrying, trying to keep the time in her mind, and slowing when she got tired.

After a while, she paused to catch her breath, and then she heard something move in the underbrush. In an instant, she dove into the bushes. She landed face-first in the dirt, and as she did a bird flew past her into the open, screeching. She scrambled into the bush, shoving aside the dense masses of branches and twigs as they lashed across her face. Nia knew she'd made too much of a racket jumping into the bush, but at least she was well concealed.

She peered out of the leaves, hardly daring to breathe. A moment later Yhui stepped out into the open. "Nia? Nia, was that you?" She called out. Nia hesitated, then crawled out of her bush and stood up. "Yes, it's me. What are you doing here?" She asked. Yhui was dressed in an outfit that looked much better equipped for a trek through the rainforest than Nia's was, and she had a pack on her back. "I came hoping you would be here. Come, follow me and I'll take you to the hideout."

She led Nia down a well-hidden path, then they arrived at a small building. It was mostly buried in the ground, so only the roof and a half-exposed window, covered in vines and dirt, could be seen. If she hadn't been looking for it Nia doubted she would've seen it. "This is it?" She asked. "Yes. There's a back entrance." Yhui said. She led her to the back of the hideout and opened a small hatch for her. Nia gave her a nod of thanks, then slipped inside. She looked around and found one guard, dead, on the floor. She sensed Yhui come inside behind her, and Nia's eyes slowly adjusted to the dim light. The only room in the small hideout was a wreck. Papers and cobwebs were strewn across the room. The cushion on the only chair had three deep gashes in its fabric, like a huge animal had sliced through it. On one of the tables lining the walls was a huge box, and where a lock should've gone there was a thin sheet of metal in the shape of a triangle. Yhui held out a hand for Nia's dagger, and she gave it to her. Yhui brushed the tip of her finger across the top of it, leaving a thin line of blood. Then she pressed her hand against the metal triangle. It glowed an ominous violet color, then the metal triangle split in half. Yhui gave Nia back her dagger, opened the box, and took out two things: a brilliant jewel, and a small jar filled with powder that Nia assumed was red moon dust. She handed them to Nia, and Nia held both of them in her arms. "Is that-?" Nia asked, breathlessly.

"Yes. The Heart of the Mountain."

The brilliant iridescent jewel reminded Nia of the fabric of time. It shimmered in the dim yellow light like light on the sea, and when Nia held it to the light a sparkling rainbow of colors exploded from it in all directions.

When Nia was finished admiring the jewel Yhui gestured for Nia to follow her, and the two of them went back through the hatch and into the open. They stood there, watching the sky start to grow lighter, and then Yhui said quietly, "I can't let you take them. They won't let me."

Nia looked down at the red moon dust and the Heart of the Mountain. She had mixed feelings about them that were hard to describe. They were both two of the most beautiful objects she had ever seen, but she couldn't imagine how hard the Paradox had fought for them and what they had sacrificed to collect them for their dark purposes. She absently reached into her satchel to touch her travel book, and paused. Her book was gone. *I must have dropped it in that bush when I dove into it,* she thought. Nia looked up at Yhui.

"What did they tell you to do?" She asked. "They told me to trap you. But I can present you with a choice." Yhui said. She took the red moon dust and the Heart of the Mountain from Nia. "Hand yourself over to the Paradox, and I'll destroy one of the ingredients for the Devastation for good." She closed her eyes. "But that means both of us will surely die."

"And if I refuse?"

"Then I'll have to take you and the ingredients by force."

"Why does the Paradox want me?" Nia asked.

"They want to keep you close because they know you could become a problem," Yhui said. "Make your choice."

The familiar effects of the contract returned, and Nia looked at Yhui with surprise. She was forced to think, but the decision didn't take her long. She handed Yhui the red moon dust. "Destroy it. But my friend Ryoko needs the Heart of the Mountain." She said. Yhui nodded, and took the jewel in one hand. There was a whiff of lavender, and it disappeared.

"Good. I returned it. Now let's hope that the Province of the Earth Spirits will keep it safer this time." Yhui said. Then Yhui held the red moon dust in her hands- and it disappeared.

Nia stared at the spot where it had been, and a realization started to creep up her.

"You didn't destroy it," Nia said. Her gaze rose to meet Yhui's. She was smiling.

And that smile was dripping with malice.

180

"Of course I didn't, sweetheart!" She said, bursting out laughing. "I love when the naive realize they've been *betrayed!*"

Chapter Fourteen
The last Phoenix!

Nia stared at her in horror.
"What did you do with it?!"
"I delivered it to Sascha, just like I did the Heart of the Mountain!"
"Sascha?"
Yhui scoffed, and took her fan from her sleeve. She fanned herself, then said, "You know him as the Great Deceiver."
"Ugh, why did I ever trust you?!"
"I told you to, didn't I?"
Nia gasped. *Of course! She did tell me to trust her, when she came to my room!*
"Traitor!" She spat.
She took a step back, and Yhui came closer.
Nia did a quick assessment. Yhui had revealed herself as an enemy. She was a powerful enemy. She had killed their

dragon taxi- and the operatives in the woods, and the guard- easily. Nia was outmatched, although she hated to admit it.

"You're really working for them?" She asked.

"Working for them? I *founded* the Paradox. Although Sascha may have helped a bit, I suppose."

"You'll never recreate the Devastation. The fabric of time and the ashes of the Phoenix-"

"Are being delivered into Paradox custody as we speak. Our operatives might be foolish minions, but they're competent foolish minions."

"What- but *how?*"

"You didn't think we were attacking the Province of the Sound Spirits for nothing, did you?"

In a flash, Nia's hands were on the hilts of her daggers.

"There's no need for violence, Nia. At least, not now. I have a job for you."

Yhui came closer, smirking. Nia took another step back.

"Do you think I'm evil?" Yhui asked, looking amused.

"Of course you are! You're trying to wipe out every living thing in Other Side!"

"Really? That may be what the Paradox is trying to do, but not me. I'll be safe and snug in the Province of the Moon Spirits while the Devastation does its work, and then-"

"Then why are you even trying to help the Paradox at all?"

"I'm not trying to help the Paradox. Creating the Paradox has simply created new opportunities for me to do the things I like most. Like the greatest game of strategy and coordination ever devised; the obliteration of a world infested with fools. Much more exciting than chess, if that's possible. Although I doubt you'll ever experience the thrill of it. And as for what I'm after... well, I'm sure you'll find out soon, won't you?"

Yhui paused, and tapped one finger on her chin thoughtfully.

"You know, all I need to do is bind you. This is really too easy."

"I dare you to try!" Nia said. She half-unsheathed her daggers, and froze when she felt a small prick in her neck.

Then the ground underneath her seemed to drop away. A throbbing dizziness rang in her head, and she touched the side of her neck. A smudge of pearlescent blood came away on her finger. She quickly sniffed it, and the familiar reek of poison jabbed through the dizzy fog of her senses. Nia groaned, and dropped to her knees.

"You're a bit slow for those daggers, aren't you?" Yhui mused, nestling her poisoned needle back into the folds of her fan. "Don't worry, sweetheart. You won't suffer for much longer."

Yhui snapped her fingers, and glowing white ropes appeared and bound Nia. Her arms were pressed to her sides and she was trapped. She couldn't move her fingers enough to reach her daggers, and even if she could, she doubted she'd be able to fight her in her foggy state. She fought against the rope, but they only grew tighter.

"Don't bother squirming. You're only the bait," Yhui said. She looked away from Nia to the forest.

Nia's eyes went wide, and she spat, *"Bait?! Bait for what?!"*

Yhui snapped her fingers again, and a gag appeared over Nia's mouth.

"I don't need to tell you anything, *prisoner."*

She went over to Nia, and grabbed her head. Then she pushed her down, forcing her to lie down. Once she was down Nia tried to sit up again, but she couldn't. She wanted to scream, but the gag made any sound she made into anguished muffled noises. Yhui knelt beside her, took a bottle from her bag, and poured the pearlescent liquid onto Nia's side. Nia froze as the warm liquid ran down her side and seeped through her clothes, and with a sick feeling, she realized that it was blood.

Then without another word, Yhui stood up and traced a wide circle on the ground around her with a piece of chalk. The outline of it glowed, then disappeared. There was a whiff of lavender, and Yhui vanished.

Nia looked around, and suddenly she was alone in the forest. She was lying in the exact center of the sun-washed clearing, and the orange light of dawn was comforting. There was no sound, but Nia's heart began to beat faster with anxiety when she remembered what Yhui had said. *The bait? What did she mean?*

She waited. She wanted to move, but she couldn't. The white ropes held her too tightly and constrained her too well. All she could do was wait. And eventually, when nothing came, she drifted off to sleep.

She woke, startled, at the sound of Enjo's voice.
"Nia!"
She looked up, and saw Enjo bursting out of the forest with Ryoko on his heels. They came to an abrupt stop when they saw the blood on Nia's side. *"No! No! Nia!"* Enjo called out. His eyes were filled with tears, and he hurried toward her. Suddenly Nia remembered the glowing circle and she wanted desperately to call out and warn Enjo. She cried out but it came out muffled. She watched terrified as Enjo and Ryoko ran into the glowing circle and knelt by her side, and she braced herself.

But nothing happened. She opened one eye and looked at Enjo and Ryoko. They were both focused on the splash of blood on Nia's side, and Enjo had already ripped open her pack and was digging through it. He was on the verge of tears. "Nia, I'm so sorry! " He wiped away the tears stinging his eyes with the back of his hand. He fished out the kit, at the same time as Ryoko ripped through the ropes. Once her arms were free Nia reached up and ripped the gag from her mouth. "I'm not hurt!" She gasped. *"It's a trap, you have to get out of here!"*

Nia mustered enough strength to sit up. Both Enjo and Ryoko looked at her in shock.

Then Enjo's eyes went wide, and his wings started to tremble. He turned to Ryoko. "Ryoko! Please, listen to me. I

186

need you to go back to the Province of the Sound Spirits now and tell them to send whatever help they can. Tell them to expect one of us to be gravely injured. *Go! Now!*"

"What?! You really expect me to run off like some coward?! I'm staying and fighting by you and Nia's sides whether you like it or not!"

"If you don't go get help, there's a chance none of us will live to see tomorrow!"

Nia's heart skipped a beat. *Tomorrow.*

She looked at the sun rising over the horizon, and her mind rewinded.

Nia muttered breathlessly, *"It's Eris' Day."*

The desperation in Enjo's voice seemed to rattle Ryoko. She swallowed grimly, and nodded. *"Fine. But if anything happens to you two,"* Ryoko paused to wipe away one of the tears that were starting to gather in the corner of her eyes. *"No. That won't happen. I'll go get help. But Enjo!"*

Enjo met her eye. A look of blazing determination had come over him, and even his wings seemed to glow with resolve.

"Take care of Nia for me. Nothing is going to stop you and Nia from seeing my acceptance ceremony into the Gatekeepers someday, especially not the Paradox. Alright?"

Enjo nodded. Ryoko gave them both one last smile, then sprinted off into the forest.

As soon as she was gone Enjo helped Nia to her feet and hugged her.

"Enjo, I'm glad you found me too, but we need to-" Nia started.

Enjo's eyes were filling with tears, and he could hardly choke his words out.

"Promise me that you'll stay happy."

"What?"

"Always take care of yourself and have good friends, and stay safe, and stay brave. Don't let the Paradox win, but if they do win, I won't be sad or blame you, okay? And Nia, I tried to be a good friend. I really tried. Oh, and one more thing,"

Enjo spoke quickly, and Nia barely had time to register what he was saying as he finished,

"Don't avenge me."

A sick feeling punched Nia in the gut. Suddenly Enjo pushed her forward and took a step back, and at that moment Nia reached out for him.

She watched in terror as Enjo coughed up blood, and the tip of a knife went through his chest.

Enjo sank to the ground, and standing behind him was Yhui. She stood there with the bloody knife in her right hand, and a satisfied look on her face. Then she glanced at Nia.

Nia couldn't think. She couldn't breathe. All of a sudden everything in her reality had stopped. When Yhui saw the expression on her face she smiled, and casually lowered the knife. Nia sunk to her knees beside Enjo.

Iridescent blood was already pooling around the wound. Her hand lifted, almost automatically, and dragged a finger across the side of her cheek. Blood came away on her fingertip. The blood Enjo had coughed up.

"Why the horrified expression, sweetie?"

Nia became dimly aware of Yhui speaking. She was starting to walk towards her, but Nia couldn't move. The moment of Enjo's murder had hit her so harshly that she hadn't even cried yet.

"Get that terrified look off your face. You look as if you've seen a ghost."

Yhui came closer. "I was trying to kill the both of you, but I suppose I'll settle for killing you one at a time," She said.

Then Yhui threw the knife, and it shot toward her for its killing blow.

Chapter Fifteen
The beginning of the end?!

Nia snapped out of her state of shock just as the tip of the knife was only inches away from her face. She realized that it'd stopped and she scrambled away out of instinct, and she stared at the hovering knife in shock.

It'd stopped in mid-air, and now it was glowing. She blinked. *No- a glowing light was resting on top of it. A glowing light the color of fire.*

The knife hovered in the light's grip, then dropped harmlessly to the ground.

The light hovered in the air for a moment, sparkling, as if it was waiting for Yhui to make her next move. Yhui stared at it in horror and shock.

Then the light flickered, and lifted, trailing sparkles of light behind it. Enjo's deathlight rose into the sky, and disappeared.

There was a moment of silence, then Yhui advanced and grabbed her knife. Nia tried to get away but a sharp pain in her chest stopped her. She groaned, remembering the poison. Then Yhui grabbed Nia's neck in one hand and threw her down, then dropped to her knees and grabbed Nia's neck in one hand, pinning her. Nia's hands went to her throat, but she felt a pinprick of pressure on the side of her neck. Yhui had the knife pressed against the side of her neck, poised to kill her at any moment.

Yhui's eyes glared down at her, burning with rage.

"I didn't come this far to let anything stop me, not even a *miracle. Now die!*"

"Stop!"

Yhui hesitated. Nia looked to the source of the sound, but there was no one there. Then, a few feet away, there was a flicker of red light. The Great Deceiver, dressed in a new elaborate grey cloak, appeared and stepped from the light.

"Yhui, you still need her."

Yhui seethed. Then she seemed to regain her posture, let go, and stand up. Nia tried to get up as well but the poison felt even stronger, ebbing through her system and snuffing out any chance of escape. "I suppose you're right, Sascha," She said, taking out her fan. "Is the Devastation nearly complete?"

"Almost," Sascha answered. He walked over to Enjo, and looked down at him. Nia forced herself to sit, and she choked out, *"Get away!"* That was all she could manage.

The idea of the Great Deceiver by Enjo's corpse sickened her.

"Now, for that feather-" The Great Deceiver knelt down, and plucked a brilliant red feather from Enjo's right wing.

Yhui gestured to Nia. Nia felt herself being lifted by magic into a standing position. "Is it time?" Yhui asked. The Great Deceiver nodded and made a complicated gesture with both hands, then Nia felt a strange trembling feeling.

She blinked, and when she opened her eyes again she gasped. Now she was standing in an open clearing surrounded by tall trees on all sides. Fog swirled around her, and when she looked down she saw her hands were now bound by tight glowing chains. All around her, arranged in a circle, were ruins. They were all huge stone pillars, and some were ensnared by vines and cracked. They were all decrepit, and Nia recognized them instantly. "The abandoned Province of the Human Spirits?" She asked aloud, breathlessly. Then something prodded her in the back, and she jumped. "Walk."

That was Yhui's voice. Nia gulped defiantly, and walked. She continued walking forward into the fog until Yhui grabbed her arm, and she stopped. Slowly the fog began to clear, and Nia gasped when a terrifying sight met her eyes. The Great Deceiver was standing over a tall pot made of glass, wearing a mask Nia knew protected against magical fumes. He was dropping the ingredients of the Devastation into the boiling water in the pot one by one, and Nia watched it turn a dull shade of grey through the clear glass of the pot. He added the Heart of the Mountain, and as the beautiful jewel melted away Nia felt sick. "It's time for the final ingredient: the future of Other Side." He said. Yhui prodded her again, and she walked forward. She glanced back at Yhui, and noticed she'd put on a mask as well. Nia walked to the pot, then Yhui took out her knife and in one motion, slid it across Nia's left arm. Nia felt its sting and flinched, then Yhui's other hand grabbed Nia's arm and thrust it over the pot. Nia's eyes stung from the fumes and watered. Through teary vision she saw her blood, pearlescent and sparkling, drip into the pot. The reaction was astonishing. The grey liquid frothed and bubbled at her blood's touch, and the entire mixture began to churn and boil. Her blood created an iridescent spiral design, then vanished.

The entire liquid stopped boiling, and now it was a darker, more sinister shade of grey. The fumes were overwhelming, and Nia felt that if she didn't move her face would melt from the heat. Yhui had relaxed her grasp, and Nia quickly moved her head from the fumes, gagging. The glass pot cracked as the liquid continued to boil, and more and more fumes rose rapidly from the pot, boiling away the mixture, until nothing was left at the bottom except four drops. These were immediately sucked out by a clear tube into a beaker and drawn into a small vial. The glass of the vial cracked immediately, but to Nia's relief, it held. The Great Deceiver disconnected the vial from the tube, then held it up. He looked at it for a moment. "Your intuition was right,

193

Yhui," he mused. "She really is the future of Other Side. And now that that's done, she can die now."

"Why bother? The surface of this world and everything on it is about to be destroyed." Yhui said, calmly.

The Great Deceiver looked to Nia. "She really is a fitting image for the future of this world. Terrorstruck, defeated-looking like she just crawled out from the future ruins of Kazaki." Nia's vision was beginning to swim, and she couldn't tell if it was from the fumes of the Devastation, the poison ebbing through her, or rage.

"It's amazing how long she's held on. What poison did you give her?" He asked. Yhui pulled the mask down from her face, and scowled. "The standard one. She *should* drop unconscious any second now."

"Oh, well. Just let me finish here, and I'll be home soon."

"Fine. Goodbye, Sascha."

Yhui turned to leave, and paused.

"You will be alright, won't you?" She asked.

"I will. You need to stop worrying so much and rest. Just leave it to me," He said.

Yhui bit her lip and furrowed her brow. Then she tossed her hair over one shoulder, and smiled. "Very well."

The Great Deceiver smiled back, and Yhui absently touched her stomach before vanishing.

Nia's heart began to beat faster. Now that Yhui was gone the chains bounding her vanished, but the Great Deceiver hadn't noticed. With his back to her he stepped forward, vial in hand. He uncorked it, and slowly began to tilt it toward the ground.

In that same instant Nia summoned the last of her energy and lunged forward, so fast that the sudden movement startled her. She snatched the vial from the Great Deceiver's hand and jumped away, and before the Great Deceiver could react more than give her a startled look she ripped the cork from the bottle. Her mind was running on adrenaline. She wasn't thinking. Instinct- or destiny- was dictating her actions.

Her father's words came back to her.

They say your mother's father- your grandad, Bakunawa- wanted the power of the Devastation for himself.

Nia watched the realization dawn on the Great Deceiver's face, and change into a look of horror.

I remember him telling me how he'd succeeded, in tying the power of the Devastation to his own magic- or more accurately, his spirit-magic.

Nia raised the vial to her lips, and squeezed her eyes shut.

He never did try it out. I guess he thought consuming the Devastation would be too risky.

All sound vanished. A petrifying taste ran down her throat.

There is one thing he mentioned, though.

The empty vial fell from her grip and landed, forgotten, on the ground.

Pain unlike anything she'd ever felt or even imagined radiated through her body, growing stronger with every pulse, an indescribable pain that filled every breath and shred of her flesh. She bent over double and fell to her knees, hugging her body to keep from ripping herself apart. *If he ever dared to drink the Devastation, he'd be given limitless power.*

Chapter Sixteen
A world upside down!

All at once, the pain stopped.

There was a moment of silence. Then, slowly, a feeling of peace fell onto Nia. She stood up, and met the eyes of the Great Deceiver. He blinked, and rage glinted in his eyes. He seemed to understand that something had happened, and somehow she was unaffected by the destructive powers of the Devastation. He advanced, unsheathing a long sword from the sheath on his belt. *"What did you just do, you little freak?!"* He howled. *"You just ruined EVERYTHING!"*

In an instant, Nia's hand pulled a dagger from its sheath and rose to block a swing from the Great Deceiver. There was the sound of grating metal, and Nia forced all her strength into pushing away the Great Deceiver's sword. Moments later they were locked in the fiercest sword fight Nia had ever fought, and she was forced to go on the defensive. Every time she blocked his sword with her daggers it'd be back for another thrust, and it was all she could manage to keep up with blocking and parrying his attacks. He thrust his sword toward her neck and she sidestepped it. She took a few steps back then lunged forward towards him, unsheathed the other dagger from its scabbard, and went to drive it deep into his side- and at that moment he slammed the pommel of his sword into her head, so hard she didn't register the pain until she stumbled and collapsed. Pain flared from the top of her skull and throbbed. Her daggers flew from her grip and landed harmlessly on the ground a few feet away.

Through spinning vision she saw the sky, then the tip of a blade. She looked up and met the Great Deceiver's malicious gaze.

Neither of them spoke for a few moments as both of them caught their breaths. Then the Great Deceiver said, through gritted teeth, "Gakusei's daughter. I remember you. I asked for your friend's death in exchange for your freedom, didn't I? Looks like you're free," He said, glancing at the palm of her right hand. The Delta was gone, but its absence made her feel sick.

The pain in Nia's skull hadn't subsided, and neither had her rage. The hatred she'd felt towards the Great Deceiver over the years felt intensified a thousand times over from seeing him in person again. Suffocating rage swelled in her chest as he continued, "You know, you're the first spirit in a long time whoever came that close to killing me," He said. His grip on the sword tightened.

Nia's life flashed before her eyes. Every happy moment, every wish for a brighter future, every kind spirit, and every tragedy passed by her like spirits walking, holding hands to guide each other through the dark.

Her love for the spirits she'd left behind overwhelmed her, and she fought back defiant tears.

"No! This isn't how it ends!"

Nia felt pressure on her neck as the Great Deceiver went to stab her throat for his killing blow, and at that moment, her mind cleared. A wave of cold washed over her and she punched the sword, so fast the sudden movement shocked her. The sword shattered. Bits of steel and ice flew, and Nia's half-closed eyes grew wide in amazement as she saw her fist. It was encased in a solid glove of ice.

The Great Deceiver stumbled backward in surprise and Nia scrambled away. She stood up uneasily and looked at her fist again, bewildered. Then Nia looked at the gash on her left arm. It was completely healed. The realization hit Nia, and she felt a smile creep up her face.

So, the realization finally set in! Welcome, Nia Angdakila, to the power of the Devastation! A familiar voice rang out in her thoughts, and she recognized it immediately. *The girl from the time bubble?* Nia wondered. To her surprise the girl responded, *Yep, it's me again. Since you drank the Devastation, your reality is* extremely *unstable. Anyway, remember how I described the time bubble as 'time is space,*

199

and space is time?' Well, the power of the Devastation is kind of like that. Anything you can imagine becomes possible! So what are you waiting for? Go beat that guy into a bloody pulp!

Nia relaxed her hand encased in ice, and the ice cracked and fell away from her fist, leaving only frost. "'Anything you can imagine becomes possible?'" Nia repeated.

She clapped her hands together. *"Then I'll push that claim to the limit!"*

She closed her eyes, concentrated her magic into her hands, and imagined. She separated her hands, and a portal grew in the gap between them. Then with one hand she drew on her spirit-magic, and grabbed onto the Great Deceiver's energy. The strange sensation of controlling another spirit entirely overwhelmed her, but she forced herself to focus. She pulled him forward, then forced him through the portal. She could look into the rift, which was quickly shifting from a window into a duplicate Other Side to a rapidly distorting rift. Through the rift was a duplicate Other Side, and all around the Great Deceiver, who was straining with pain under Nia's spirit-magic, the instability of the duplicate universe was clear. Nia clapped her hands together. In the rift, somewhere far in the distance, there was a rumble like distant thunder.

Nia saw Other Side compressing itself, pushing all the empty space onto itself, coming closer. The ground began to shake uncontrollably.

She could feel her victory coming closer, and a smile crept up her face.

She paused, and slowly brought her hands together. The rumbling grew louder, and stopped.

For a moment, nothing moved.

Then the rift snapped shut, and all that was left of the Great Deceiver was an anguished scream that rang out long after the rift had vanished.

After the sound had subsided Nia looked to the sky, and felt the first raindrops of a storm fall onto her face. The sky darkened, and thunder crashed.

"*Orenda,*" Nia murmured.

She took a step back to bask in her victory, and gagged.

The world was spinning again, and she could taste blood in her mouth. Nia put a hand on her heart, and froze. Her heart wasn't beating. A clammy feeling of panic grabbed her. What had the Devastation done to her? Had it fried her insides so badly that everything inside her was ash? Were these her dying moments? She groaned, and coughed up more blood. *At least,* she thought as the world faded to black, *I stopped the Paradox.*

Chapter Seventeen
Home again!

Nia opened her eyes to rippling light. She gasped, and inhaled water. It was warm and left the faint taste of herbs on her tongue. Panic set in immediately. *I'm in water. Where am I? Must get out of the water!*

She sat up so fast it startled her. Blinding pain and soreness flared across her body like all of her bones were exploding into fireworks. Light dazzled her eyes. She groaned, and a few excruciating seconds later, the pain subsided and her eyes adjusted. Her first thought was, *Am I dead?*

Smiling back at her was her mother and father. A moment of silence passed as the three of them looked at each other, their eyes full of relief and the indescribable joy of seeing someone you thought you lost.

They looked exactly like how Nia had remembered them. Her mother still had a head full of curly brown hair and a caring look in her eye, and her father in his human form still had his powder blue hair cut short. But both of them looked more tired and thin than she'd ever seen them before.

Her mother was the first to react. She reached a hand to brush Nia's hair from her eyes, and smiled. "Nia?"

Nia held her mother's hand, and resisted the urge to burst into happy tears.

"Mama? Dad?"

The next ten minutes were full of hugs, happy tears, and after telling each other how much they'd missed each other at least a dozen times, catching up. As Nia's parents told her everything that had happened to them, and how they'd been freed from the inescapable prison they'd been sentenced to only three days ago, it was still hard to believe they were really there.

"What was the prison like?" Nia asked.

Her parents shuddered, and a hollow look came into their eyes. Nia's mother shook her head. "Nightmarish," She said. "We tried every day to escape, but we couldn't."

"Not until an army of spirits stormed the place, at least. Turns out with the all the Paradox members scattered and their leader gone, someone *finally* figured out where the prison was." Her father added, bitterly.

"What happened to you those years? Were you hurt?" Nia's mother asked.

Nia told them both everything: how she'd been forced to join the Paradox, all the missions she'd gone on, how she and Enjo had escaped, how they'd met Ryoko, and finally, how she'd stopped the Great Deceiver. She left out the part about Enjo's death. Although she wanted to tell them, whenever she tried her throat tensed and she couldn't force out a word without tearing up. When she was finished her parents stared back at her in wonder. Then they smiled. "I'm proud of you, kiddo," her dad said. Nia smiled back, and glanced down. For the first time she realized that she'd been sitting in a rectangular pool of water, and whenever she moved, her legs brushed against miniature lily pads and tiny fish and frog-fairies dotting the water's surface. She was wearing a white patient's dress, and when she looked at the room around her she realized she was in a large, elegant suite. In one corner of the room, a bat-cat Cuddly was sitting in a pet bed, licking itself.

"Wait, where am I?" She asked. There was the sound of an explosion and cheering outside, and she caught a glimpse of a bright light through a sliding door at the far end of the room. "And what was that?" She added.

"We're in a hospital in Kazaki. Ryoko Bayani went back to the Province of the Sound Spirits for help, and they brought you here. When we escaped we were told you were here, so we came here and we've been waiting for you to wake up since." Her mother said. "And as for that," Her father said, gesturing to beyond the sliding door, "Are you feeling fine enough to walk?"

Nia's mother shot him a warning glance, but before she could speak Nia had already uneasily got to her feet in the pool. Every movement was agony, but once she stood, the pain disappeared. "Yes, I feel fine. I want to come see."

Her parents helped her out of the pool, and after drying herself with her water magic, Nia walked with them to the sliding door. Her father slid it open, and the three of them walked out into the night.

After her eyes adjusted to the darkness, Nia gasped. Above them a red firework exploded, then two others leaped into the air and burst into streamers of light. They were standing on a balcony, and below them Nia could see Kazaki's Ceremonial Square. She'd been to the Ceremonial Square before, but she'd never seen it so full of spirits. There must've been hundreds of spirits in the huge crowd below them. And after every bang of a firework there was a collective cheer, flags and confetti flew, and paper lanterns shaped as blossoms floated into the sky. More fireworks leaped into the air, lighting up the entire Ceremonial Square and the skyscrapers lining it in shades of festive color.

Nia felt her heart swell with silent wonder and joy, and a smile crept up her face.

"Enjoying the celebrations?" Her mother asked. "Yes. Very much," Nia said, breathlessly. "It's a good thing Eris' Day celebrations go on for a week. Otherwise, you would've missed it... and *this!*" Her father made a dramatic gesture, and there was the smell of seaweed as a stick with chunks of fried dough skewered onto it magically appeared in his hand. He offered it to Nia, and she took it. "It's called sugar cakes on a stick! I bought it from a vendor on the way here. Like it?" He asked. She looked at it for a moment, then sunk her teeth into the warm dough of one of the cakes. The sugar sprinkled onto it melted on her tongue, and she swallowed. "Yes, it tastes amazing. Thank you," she said. She looked down at the sugar cakes to take another bite, and froze. She noticed for the first time a jet-black scar on the back of her left hand, and her heart filled with horror as her eye followed the black scar up her arm to her left shoulder. She looked at both of her parents in shock, and they looked back at her grimly. "The doctors say they think it's a side effect of the power of the Devastation. They say it healed your arm, but it left that scar in the process. As soon as I get the chance, I'm going to write to your grandad and see what other 'side effects' drinking the Devastation might have," Her mother said. Nia blinked in surprise. "Granddad? Isn't he still-?"

"Yes. But he's about to wake up."

Nia's eyes widened.

"What? After all this time?"

Her mother nodded. "We just got the news today. He's about to wake up, and so are the rest of the Ancient Spirits. And when they do, they'll have news for us. All we can do is hope that it's good news."

At that moment the door to the room behind them swung open, and two spirits rushed inside. The first was a Harpy woman with long white hair and a frantic look in her eyes. The Earth Spirit behind her was clearly a nurse, and when they entered both of them rushed to the three on the balcony and started speaking at once.

"Mr. and Mrs. Angdakila, I tried to tell her that Nia needed her rest-"

"Nia? Nia! Are you alright? I'm sorry for bursting in like this, but I-"

Nia's mother shot the nurse a look, silencing her. "She's fine. You're dismissed," she said to the nurse. The nurse silently obeyed, and a moment later the door shut behind her. When she was gone Nia looked at the Harpy woman, and recognized her immediately. *"Mrs. Snowy?"* She gasped. Enjo's mother looked so thin and stressed it was frightening. Her white hair was tied in a disheveled side braid, the elegant green dress she wore couldn't hide the visible bones in her ribs and arms, and her face, which Nia had remembered as looking sweet and kind, looked hollow and sickly pale. Snowy curtsied, then sat on her knees and bowed her head in respect. "Nia, a girl named Ryoko Bayani told me everything. For the last two years, I've suffered knowing there was nothing I could do to see or help my son." Her wings, which were covered in feathers that resembled a peacock's, went limp. When she looked up again her eyes were swelling with tears. *"Please, what happened to Enjo?"* She pleaded.

There was a short silence. Snowy and her parents looked at her intently.

Nia's mouth went dry. Her mind raced for an answer, but all she could think of was how Snowy would react if she knew the truth. *Burst into tears? Drop dead?*

Both of these seemed likely. A few moments passed, and Nia felt her throat tense as she made her choice.

"He's alive."

Snowy's eyes lit up with renewed hope, and her parents gave sighs of relief.

"Where is he?" Snowy asked, getting to her feet. Nia shrugged. "I don't know," She said, as a feeling of guilt began to grow in her gut. "I last saw him in the   Malaka Rainforest. I have no idea what happened to him, after I blacked out."

"Then I'm going to go find him. Thank you for everything, Nia," Snowy said. She hurried to the door, but stopped in the doorway at the sound of Nia's mother's voice. "Snowy, at least get your strength back before you go." She said. Snowy shook her head. "I'll pack food for the journey, but I can't waste any more time," She said. She closed the door behind her, and the guilty feeling in Nia's gut grew.

Later that night, after Nia's mother had convinced her to spend a little more time in the healing pool and given her a new outfit to wear, Nia and her parents left the hospital and joined the crowd in the Ceremonial Square. The crowd of celebrating spirits seemed even larger here, and it was difficult to be heard over the pounding music, laughter, and cheering. Nia and her parents found a place to sit in a cheery ramen stall, and as they dug into the first real meal Nia had eaten in days, she heard the flutter of fabric as someone ducked inside behind them. She turned to look, and almost dropped her fork when she saw Ryoko.

Ryoko seemed just as shocked, but she recovered quickly. "Nia! You're safe!" She said. Before Nia could react Ryoko grabbed her in a fierce bear hug from behind. "I'm so glad you're alright! When we couldn't find you or Enjo in the forest we went to the Province of the Human Spirits as fast as we could, because the Geeta got one of the Superiors to cough up where they'd be brewing the Devastation-"

"Ryoko-"

"And *then* when we found you there, I thought you were *dead!* And we couldn't find the Great Deceiver anywhere! *I was freaking out!*"

"Ryoko, you're crushing me-"

"And *then* I thought, 'Well, the Sound Spirits have great doctors, they'll heal her quickly,' but *then* you had to be transported to Kazaki for specialty treatment! *Fast! I thought you were going to die! We were so worried!*"

"I think I'm dying-"

"But since you're here now, I guess you're fine!" Ryoko said. She paused when she caught sight of Nia's ramen, and her eyes went wide. "Oh! Nice! What kind of ramen is that? I'm starving." She let go of Nia and sat down beside her. Nia gasped for air. "A number twelve, please," Ryoko said, addressing the cook behind the counter. There was another fluttering sound as the fabric hanging down from the ceiling of the shop parted, and another spirit stepped inside. It was Rashidi, and when he caught sight of Nia's father he stopped.

"Gakusei?"

"Rashidi?"

Rashidi sat down beside Ryoko, and as he and Nia's dad started chatting, Nia realized something.

"Ryoko, wait… you said you couldn't find Enjo in the forest?"

The cook placed a bowl of steaming ramen in front of Ryoko, and she licked her lips eagerly. "Hm? No, of course not. The Geeta said he was missing, so some search parties were sent out to find him," She answered. Ryoko slurped a long noodle, and after noticing the bewildered look in Nia's eye asked, "What?"

"N-nothing," Nia said. The cook placed a bowl of ramen in front of her, and she ate it in silence.

"Oh! That reminds me, Ryoko. I want you to have this." Rashidi said. He turned to his daughter and gave her a kind smile, then took something small from his pocket, and placed it in her palm. Ryoko's eyes went wide with astonishment.

"A Gatekeeper's badge? But dad, I'm not-"

"You are now. After everything you've told me, you've more than earned the title of Gatekeeper; but you'll have to do some training it's official," He said. Ryoko's eyes lit up, and it looked like her eyes would well up with happy tears at any moment. *"Thanks, Dad."* She said.

A few minutes later, all five of them were finished with their ramen. They left the shop to watch the fireworks, and a few minutes later Nia's dad led them through an executive building to another private balcony overlooking the crowd.

As Nia watched the beautiful sparks of color rain down from above, she leaned against the balcony's railing. She watched another firework bloom, and realized this would be a moment she would remember for the rest of her life. Nia gave a contented smile.

Rest in peace, Enjo, She thought. *I wish you could be here.* She watched a paper lantern in the shape of a tiny blossom float up to the balcony, and she cupped it in her hand. *We did it. We saved Other Side. And I know you're happy, for everyone. You're wiser than I ever imagined you to be.* She silently blew the small blossom from her hand, and it floated upwards, to the sky. She watched it go, and looked to either side of her. On one side of her were her parents, and on the other side was Ryoko and her father. They were all looking up in quiet wonder at the fireworks. *I won't let your sacrifice be for nothing, Enjo. I'll stay brave. I'll stay happy.*

Nia looked back to the sky just in time to see the grand finale.

And I'll live out every minute of the rest of my life- the best story from Other Side that I know.

Chapter Eighteen
Happy endings and why we want them!

The Paradox had failed, but the true battle had been won.
With the Devastation and Sascha gone, the members of the Paradox were quickly scattered. But that hardly mattered now. For Yhui, the key to everything she'd ever wanted was, quite literally, in her hands.

She groaned, and dragged the black sack into the main room of her tower. Moonlight was shining through the main window, throwing squares of light onto the wooden planks. She dragged the sack into the center of the light, and looked around. *"Zahquere!"* She snapped. *"Where are you?"*

There was the scampering sound of paw steps, then a dog peeked out from behind one of the doors built into the dark bookshelves lining the room. His body was covered with beautiful blue fur that shone like the cosmos. His ears were oversized, and he looked cuter than physically possible. "Yes, Mrs. Yhui?" He asked.

"Prepare the examination table," Yhui said. She sunk into an armchair and watched Zahquere scamper around the room, pulling out a wooden table with his magic. When he was finished he stood at attention, and looked at Yhui expectantly.

"Open the bag, and put it on the table," Yhui instructed. Zahquere went over to the bag, and opened it at the top. His eyes widened, but he didn't say anything. Then with an ease that was surprising for his small size, lifted out the bag's contents with his magic and uneasily set it on the table. With a gleam in her eye, Yhui crossed over to the table and examined her prize. The corpse looked stiff and pale in the white moonlight. It was hard to imagine that it had ever been alive, and Yhui had to reach out and run her fingers through its hair to convince herself it was really there.

Zahquere gagged. "That smell- *it's horrible!* How long has it been dead?" He gasped.

"Only three days. I would've retrieved it sooner, but I was tied up celebrating Eris' Day with my family in the Province," Yhui answered.

"It's in pretty good condition for a corpse that's only been dead three days. But what happened to its chest?" Zahquere asked. Judging by the hesitation in his voice, he seemed afraid to know the answer.

"Completely charred. Must've burst into flame."

Zahquere's nose wrinkled with disgust.

"And how did it *die?*" He asked.

Yhui didn't answer. Instead, she snapped her fingers, and Zahquere stood at attention.

"Bring me the book."

Zahquere stepped out of the moonlight, and reappeared a few moments later with a thin book in his mouth. It was so ragged and covered with dirt and creases that the title was hardly visible. Yhui took it, and flipped to its first pages. She scanned over the words, and a satisfied smile crept up her face. Yhui snapped the book closed, and gently set it on the corpse's stomach. Zahquere read the title of the book out loud, inquisitively, "*'Travel Guide to Other Side?'*" Then he added, "Never much cared for it." Yhui scoffed.

"You can hardly *imagine* the things I've sacrificed to get that book."

"Can't you buy a copy at a bookstore for twenty-four blissies? I could hardly call that a sacrifice-"

Yhui gave him a freezing glare, and he went quiet.

"That copy, *Zahquere,* is the only one of its kind. It's the last surviving possession of Eris herself."

At the word *Eris,* a cold draft blew across the floor, chilling Zahquere's paws and filling him with a sense of dread he didn't understand. He watched uneasily as Yhui arranged the corpses' hands over the book and turned to him. "Now, before I go on, I suppose I owe you an explanation so you know how I expect you to act when she arrives," Yhui said.

Zahquere blinked. "What? Someone's coming to visit? *At this hour?*" He asked, nervously. "But I haven't put a kettle on!"

"Come. Sit."

Yhui sat down in the armchair, and Zahquere hurried over. He sat expectantly on its ottoman. Yhui patted her lap, and he happily climbed onto it. She stroked his fur, and Zahquere remembered the happy times he'd spent like this as a puppy: curled in Yhui's lap, getting stroked and scratched behind the ears for hours while she read book after book. He could tell Yhui was trying hard to contain herself, but she was practically shaking with excitement.

"Do you remember my main project, Zahquere?" She asked.

"Of course."

"Well, I realized that for me to continue with it I would need an ally. But the only spirit that could help me had vanished off the face of Other Side long ago. From my research I guessed she existed somewhere I could never reach, so I had to bring her to me." Yhui continued stroking Zahquere's fur, and he wondered how this story would eventually lead to the corpse lying on the table only a few feet away. "With Sascha's assistance, I formed the Paradox. With him taking on the mask of the Paradox's true leader I was free to remain behind the scenes, as I preferred," Yhui went on. "Sascha insisted on letting the Paradox and its members pursue other goals, so I allowed it. Under Sascha's guidance, the Paradox went on to, in a sense, conquer Other Side. But I never cared for any of their petty schemes.

215

I was always focused on the Paradox's true goal, and how it would ultimately contribute to my main project. I spent years researching and planning the best way to recreate the Devastation, as I'd read the Devastation was necessary to summon the spirit I needed."

"But who were they?" Zahquere asked.

"Eris, the forgotten Ancient Spirit of Chaos."

Zahquere's eyes went wide. *"A forgotten Ancient Spirit?"* He asked, hardly daring to believe it.

"Yes, one of the most powerful spirits Other Side will ever know, and a spirit so well buried in history spirits remember little of her except her name and a teaching tale. With the Paradox's infinite resources at my disposal, I soon learned that I needed three things to summon Eris: first, the Devastation, because its raw power came close to how much power she'd had when she was alive. Second, her favorite possession, to call back her spirit. And last of all, the perfect vessel. It had to be the body of a spirit, and only the most powerful type of spirit could hope to withstand Eris' power... a Hawkee."

Zahquere gasped. "So the corpse, it's a Hawkee?"

"Yes. He was a boy named Enjo Kutana, but that hardly matters now. Anyway, one miracle after another, fate played out in my favor. Enjo Kutana was hatched and became the first Hawkee to walk Other Side in two hundred years. The Ancient Spirit of Time gave the fabric of time to a talented young fashion designer. The Paradox, who'd been keeping most of the former members of the Assembly hostage, managed to collect all of the Spirit Leaders' blood and secure the 'past' of Other Side. I realized only the Paradox could be the 'present' of Other Side, and ingeniously created the magic contracts. New and old members of the Paradox were forced to fill a small vial with their blood and sign their contract with it. Little did the operatives know, the blood that remained in the vial after the contract was signed was stored and ultimately used as the 'present' ingredient in the Devastation."

Zahquere, who knew the ingredients to the Devastation by heart, asked, "What about the future of Other Side? How did you guess that?"

Yhui paused, and gave him a mysterious smile, "I have my ways. I learned the daughter of Gakusei and Yuriko symbolized the future of Other Side, and I ordered her and Enjo Kutana to join the Paradox by any means, so they would be close by when I needed them."

"But why would that girl symbolize the future of Other Side?" Zahquere asked.

"Destiny works in… unique ways. But after many years of preparing, I was ready to begin the process of creating the Devastation, and become one step further to completing my main project. When Enjo and the girl Nia turned fifteen-"

"Why wait until they're fifteen, Mrs. Yhui?" Zahquere interrupted.

"Because that's the age when a Hawkee's inner core, or the internal source of their Fire Magic, stabilizes. If I'd killed him any earlier he would've just exploded, and that wouldn't do." She closed her eyes thoughtfully, then went on. "Anyway, I sent a letter to their caretaker, ordering her to hand them over to me. She refused, and I suspected she'd grown attached to them. So I sent operatives disguised as thieves to retrieve the Hawkee and the girl, but Namei killed the operatives before they got the chance. And so, I was forced to think of another solution. As I was trying to think of another way to get them in my power a Superior mentioned that he'd ordered Namei to kill the kids if they ever learned the truth about the Paradox, saying he didn't think they should suffer knowing the truth. I was outraged at the time, but then I realized that could work out in my favor,"

She paused and held out her hand. There was a whiff of lavender as she worked her magic, and a glass of icy water appeared in her hand. She took a long sip before continuing.

"I took some records from the Superiors' and Sascha's files, and let them fall into the hands of untrustworthy operatives. Sure enough, they stole the records and went rogue, and I immediately assigned Nia, Enjo, and Namei to track them down. Again fate worked out in my favor, and Nia and Enjo learned the truth. It ended with Nia and Enjo on a pathetic quest to stop the Paradox, and Namei's corpse at the bottom of a Kazaki canal. All was well."

"What happened next?"

"To make a long story short, Nia and Enjo ended up collecting two of the irreplaceable ingredients of the

Devastation. I 'happened' to cross paths with them, and when I did all it took was a bit of Blood Magic to earn their trust. I knew I couldn't steal the ingredients from them without losing the trust I'd just earned- which could prove valuable in the long run- so I waited. They told me how they planned to hand the ashes of the Phoenix and the fabric of the time over to Geeta Sebanu for him to protect. I knew I couldn't waste a moment, so later that day I hurried back to the Paradox headquarters and orchestrated a full-scale attack against the Province of the Sound Spirits. The operatives and Superiors of the Paradox attacked, and a handful of the Paradox's most skilled members were able to steal the ashes of the Phoenix and the fabric of time from Geeta Sebanu. After that, I delivered two other ingredients to Sascha, killed the Hawkee, captured the girl, and in a moment of triumph, Sascha and I recreated the Devastation."

Zahquere looked up at her in awe. Yhui took another long sip, and went on. "Everything was going well, until I decided to let Sascha handle the rest. I went back to the Palace of the Moon Spirits to relax, and an hour later learned that Sascha had failed."

"Yes, you were *quite* angry."

"And rightfully so! I thought my life's work had been ruined, until I came back to the abandoned Province of the Human Spirits and found the corpse of the Hawkee, and the smallest drop remaining in the vial of the Devastation. I knew destiny had come through for me again."

"Was the girl there?" Zahquere asked.

"No. She must have survived the effects of the Devastation, because any trace of her was gone. But I found her travel book nearby, and at last, after all these years, I have *everything* I need to make my dreams come true."

Zahquere was quiet for a moment. Then he asked, "Mrs. Yhui, where's Sascha?"

"He's fine. I know what happened to him, and he should be back shortly," She said, dismissively.

"But Mrs. Yhui, what about the…?"

There was a brief silence. Then Yhui looked away from him and said, "He'll be back in time."

She stood up abruptly, and Zahquere tumbled off her lap. Yhui hurried over to the table and snapped, "I expect you to be on your best behavior when Eris arrives! So when she's here, don't say a word!"

She took a small vial out of the pocket of her dress. In the fleeting moment she held it out and poured out its contents the cracks crisscrossing the vial shone in the moonlight, and Zahquere wondered if someone had dropped it. A tiny drop fell onto the book, and the cold draft returned. It blew across the floor, throwing open the book to its final, empty pages.

Glowing words written in a language Zahquere couldn't understand appeared on the pages, and a moment later, the wind ceased. The words vanished.

And all was quiet.

Zahquere released a breath he didn't know he'd been holding, and gave a sigh of relief.

"Was something supposed to happen?" He asked, looking up at Yhui.

She was staring down at the corpse in shock and disbelief. After a moment tears of rage gathered in her eyes, and she shrieked, *"No! No! This has to work!"*

Zahquere quickly took a few steps backward. But in his hurry his paw hit something, and he yelped. He collapsed onto the floor, and Yhui turned quickly to look. The wrath in her eyes vanished, and she hurried over. She silently helped him up, then looked him over. "You're not hurt," She said, flatly. Then she walked back over to the table, and with her back to him, began to sob. Zahquere silently went to stand next to her, and rested his head against her side. Yhui automatically petted him, and they stood in silence.

After a few minutes, Zahquere silently offered her a handkerchief. She accepted, and dabbed her eyes. A few moments of silence passed, then Yhui's eyes lit up. She rushed over to the spot where Zahquere had tripped, and picked up a huge leather-bound journal. She hurried back over to the table and flipped through the pages, and with an excited gleam in her eyes flipped to the last page. *"I'd nearly forgotten,"* She said, breathless with new hope. "Forgotten what?" Zahquere asked. "The phrase! To summon her!" Yhui snapped. "Now please be quiet. This phrase is old as Other Side itself, and bodes more evil than all its monsters combined," She said. Zahquere nodded, and took a step back. Yhui cleared her throat, and said in a clear, forced voice, "'What could go wrong?'"

Acknowledgments

I'd like to thank my family, especially my mom and dad, who've always been supportive of my dream of becoming an author. Mom, thank you for everything you've done to nurture my journey as a writer. Dad, thank you for always supporting me and always being excited to read what I've written next. You two exposed me to some of the greatest storytelling I know and kept me motivated to finish this book. Thank you so much!

I'd also like to thank my writing teacher, Ms. Becca. I learned a lot in your class, and the weekly writing sessions with my classmates was like rocket fuel for my imagination.

Thanks to everyone who contributed to this book, and helped my dream become a reality.

About the Author

Malaya Wakefield is a gifted new voice in the genre of fantasy whose charming characterization, quirky worlds that celebrate her diverse ancestry, and prose full of heart and humor stand out from the crowd. She is a part-time daydreamer and author of the groundbreaking YA fantasy series "Stories From Other Side."